October Kiss

Based on the Hallmark Channel Original Movie

Kristen Ethridge

October Kiss
Copyright @ 2018 Crown Media Publishing LLC

Print ISBN: 978-1-947892-36-1
Ebook ISBN: 978-1-947892-29-3

Hallmark
PUBLISHING

www.hallmarkpublishing.com
For more about the movie visit:
www.hallmarkchannel.com/october-kiss

Chapter One

FALL IN SEATTLE NEVER DISAPPOINTED Poppy
Summerall. The air around Puget Sound felt
crisp and clear as it tickled the leaves of the
dense foliage all around the Pacific Northwest. The
leaves on the trees showed off, trumpeting their colors
in a visual symphony of deep orange and burning red
and shocking gold.

Kids around the area had already headed back to
school. The salmon in the local streams had begun to
jump their way back to the waters they'd once called
home. And fall festivals began to set up operations,
full of apples and corn and pumpkins.

Poppy considered pumpkins to be her favorite. She
loved them not just because they signaled the warmth
and joy of spending time with family for the upcoming
holiday season. They also reminded her of the fun and
silliness of Halloween, of costumes and pretend, of
candy and cookies. They reminded her of a time in
her childhood that wasn't tainted with the heartbreak
of her parents' divorce. Halloween had always been a

moment on the calendar where she could indulge her free spirit and just be.

Halloween got Poppy. It knew everyone just needed a time for fun in their lives.

Halloween understood that no one could be serious all the time.

Poppy knew that, too. Unfortunately, adulting and paying bills on time and all the other things that signaled membership in the ranks of being a grown-up didn't always respect Poppy's need to be her own person, or her struggles to find her own way.

Her mind wandered as she brought her yoga class to the heart of their day's practice. Why couldn't things be like Halloween and yoga—fun, accompanied by a chance to go with the flow?

"Good, everybody. Full plank. Good. Belly towards your spine. And now we're going to lower down and come up into what I like to call…*sssssssnake*."

Poppy touched her stomach and chest to her mat, then tucked her elbows beside her and pushed her torso upwards. No one laughed at her slithering reptile impression.

Didn't anyone have fun anymore?

She decided to ignore the slightly confused stares from the attendees of the yoga class dotted around the grass in front of her. "There's this great yoga word for this pose…but I can't remember what it is. It kinda sounds like a sneeze. It's like…asnasnanataaaa…aaahnnnnaaaaanana."

A voice came from the front row as Poppy pulled

up to one knee, then lifted her arms to the puffy white clouds above.

"Anjaneyasana."

"Anjaneyasana!" Of course. That was it. Poppy couldn't believe she hadn't been able to remember it. For all her thoughts about silliness the last few minutes, forgetting that crazy yoga word took the cake. "Thank you, Mrs. Klemmer."

"And you have to make sure you keep your knee over your ankle, so you don't damage your patella," Mrs. Klemmer continued.

Really, Mrs. Klemmer sounded so much better at this gig than Poppy.

Poppy loved the freedom of yoga, but the instruction part—the part where you had to make sure everyone and everything was lined up right—that always felt difficult. She couldn't *just be* while teaching yoga. She had to *be on*. As she thought about it, Poppy began to realize that maybe teaching these yoga classes in the park wasn't going to be the career path for her. These students deserved someone who was committed to their instruction, someone whose strength was in deepening their practice. Poppy loved yoga and she loved being out here teaching, but she questioned everything these days. Even what she was doing right this moment.

What if Poppy's biggest concern was to get some exercise outside while breathing the fresh fall air—not thinking about patellas? What would that mean for these folks? Suddenly, Poppy's mind began to whirl.

"Oh." She beckoned Mrs. Klemmer up to the front mat. "Do you want to come up and show us?"

Mrs. Klemmer's graying ponytail jiggled slightly at the nape of her neck as she nodded and jogged up to where Poppy was standing.

"Great." Poppy stepped aside and watched as the older woman knelt low into the pose, then stretched each arm tall alongside her ears.

She looked precise. She looked focused. She looked like a real yoga teacher.

"Knee. Over. The. Ankle. Arms up in the air. Anjaneyasana." She leaned forward, swooping down to rest her hands lightly on the mat before transitioning into the next pose. "Warrior two."

Mrs. Klemmer showed the poise of a true yogi.

In comparison, Poppy felt more like Yogi Bear.

"Um…Mrs. Klemmer?" Poppy dropped her voice to a whisper as Mrs. Klemmer continued through the salutation.

"Yeah?" The older woman never broke stride.

"You're very good at this. Do you want to take over the class?"

Mrs. Klemmer turned her head slightly to acknowledge Poppy's question. "Oh. Sure. Of course."

It seemed like Mrs. Klemmer wasn't even shocked by Poppy bringing the idea up.

"Really? That would be great." Poppy thought the feeling that washed over her was relief. But she wasn't entirely certain.

"Okay."

Was Poppy's inadequacy as a yoga instructor that apparent? Well, this pretty much indicated that she could scratch anything instructionally-based off the list of potential careers...

"I'm gonna go."

Mrs. Klemmer's perfect rhythm of inhaling and exhaling never varied. "Okay. Bye."

"I'm just gonna get my bag." Poppy contorted herself underneath the teacher's outstretched arm and snatched the leather duffel off the ground. "Thank you."

There was nothing left to do but race away from the class and far from her latest failed career incarnation.

Later that afternoon, Poppy's journey to adulting didn't get any smoother. She'd been working at Marino's Pizza Parlor near the University of Washington campus for about a month to put a little regular money in her bank account until the number of yoga students at her classes picked up. She'd hoped to build a base of clients who would recommend her, so she could then start charging for the classes and maybe find her place in Seattle.

At first, the management at Marino's put her on the register while another team member was out taking care of a sick grandmother. But when Monica came back, Jimmy, the manager, transferred Poppy to the kitchen.

Today was her third day as a chef—so to speak— and Poppy could honestly say it was her third day of disaster. Yesterday, she'd tripped and knocked a pizza off the peel. It slid so far back into the depths of the brick oven that Jimmy wasn't able to retrieve it before it became a charred circle of doom.

So far, nothing she'd made was going to inspire any fancy reviews on Yelp. But at least tossing dough in the air spoke to her carefree side.

Until she lost control of the disc of pizza dough in the air, and it came darned close to landing smack on her face. Poppy stuck her hands up to catch the dough, but instead it hit her fingers and tore. Poppy realized that—much like the yoga classes—her zen wasn't going to be found in pizza either.

"I'm sorry, Jimmy. I don't think I'm very good at this."

Jimmy's brow furrowed as he studied the sad result of her efforts. "It happens."

Poppy lifted her blue apron from atop her Marino's-issued green polo shirt. Her zen clearly wasn't going to be found in synthetic fabrics, either. She wadded the apron in a ball and handed it to Jimmy.

"Now that you're free, I was wondering if maybe we could go out sometime." Jimmy looked a bit like a lovestruck teenager.

What was that song about moons and pizza pies? It seemed to be coming to life, right here in Marino's.

Poppy's mouth went dry. Wasn't he supposed to tell her something about when she could come pick up her last check? Or, like, a reference or something? When did asking ex-employees out become part of the termination process?

"Oh…I don't date my bosses." The very thought made her feel icky. She could use something that centered her right about now. Too bad nothing in her life was working today. Not teaching yoga. Not pizza-making. And definitely not dating. Because she wasn't going on a date with Jimmy.

Jimmy fired back with a practical observation. "Great. Because I'm not your boss anymore."

"Or my ex-boss." She knew she hadn't let him down easy, but she didn't really care. She needed to get out of Marino's. She needed to take several deep breaths of the fall Seattle air.

Poppy grabbed a "Help Wanted" sign from under the counter and stuck it up to display on the kitchen's countertop. Hopefully, the speed with which she walked away, never looking back, would make her point—about both her skills as a pizza chef and her unavailability as a potential date.

Adulting was hard. And, quite possibly, not for Poppy.

Nightfall didn't make the day any better.

In a weak moment last week, Poppy had agreed to let her sister, Megan, set her up on a blind date. Megan's husband had recently been deployed for six months from the nearby naval station in Everett. Megan had moped around for the first few weeks, and Poppy finally caved on this blind date thing because she'd thought it would make her sister happy.

When it came to Megan, Poppy would do just about anything. They'd been a dynamic duo for years, navigating weekends shuttled back-and-forth from one parent to the other. Poppy never would have made it without Megan, and she loved her sister with a fierceness that she often found hard to put into words.

Which is how she found herself doing the one thing she swore she'd never do again: letting someone fix her up on a date.

It wasn't that Poppy didn't believe in true love. She did. She really did. All she had to do was look at Megan and Gary to know that real, genuine love was out there. But like so many things, every time Poppy tried it, it went wrong.

Dates don't always have to end in disaster, right? Poppy gave herself a mental pep talk as she watched tonight's candidate for happily-ever-after, Mike, come up the front sidewalk. Besides, Megan knew Mike from the navy. He had to be a good guy if he sailed out on the high seas to defend America.

Poppy nodded, pleased with her own internal realization. She took a deep breath, then opened the door before Mike even knocked. She *could* do this.

He came inside for a moment and said hi to Megan as they exchanged initial pleasantries—Poppy felt pleased to notice nothing had seemed too awkward so far.

"Let me take your arm," Mike said as they walked out. He smelled good. His cologne was manly. It smelled like something a guy who had a career defending his country would wear. He looked nice, too—he had a little bit of gel in his dark hair to sculpt it back.

Poppy noticed that even his clothes seemed to be ironed. He'd put in some effort for their evening out. You didn't really see that much anymore. In a world of Tinder swiping, Mike might just be a Cyrano de Bergerac.

"Thank you." She tucked her hand in the bend of his elbow. So far, so good. "What a gentleman. So, what are we doing tonight?"

Mike smiled down at her as he squeezed her hand. Poppy wanted to deny that she liked the way the closeness felt, but she couldn't. She didn't want to get too far ahead of herself, but this was nice. It seemed like they were part of a team. Team Date.

She liked the sound of that. She'd never been much for sports, but she could find a way to get used to this kind of team.

"Tonight is dinner at a romantic little spot off the beaten track—the best food in the city."

Poppy's heart fluttered a little, the pit-pat of butterfly wings reinforcing what the lightning-quick thought in her mind had already told her. Not only had he ironed his pants, he'd thought about where they would eat. He'd planned this. He'd been looking forward to tonight and wanted to make it special.

And all the while, she'd been sulking because she'd been fixed up on another blind date. She'd assumed this would be one more dead end.

Well, shame on her. Shame on her for believing the worst about Mike before she'd ever met him. Shame on her for automatically writing off this date just because every other first date in her life had gone like the comic relief scene midway through a chick flick.

Tonight would be different. "That sounds great."

Poppy meant every word she said. Mike's plan did sound great. And it felt great to be positive and relaxed about tonight.

Maybe Mike was her zen.

"Yeah, then tomorrow I was thinking breakfast in the country with my mother—she's very excited to meet you. Are you a size two? Because if you are, her wedding dress would be a perfect fit. We've got enough time to get in a spring wedding—I think it will be too humid here in July."

Poppy pulled away, like a wayward thread unraveling the closeness she'd felt between them a moment ago.

"How do you feel about big families? My mother loves them. That's why I'm the middle of five boys. I've always wanted a big family, too. Five worked for my parents. I think it will work for me, too. What do you say?"

Nothing. Poppy said nothing.

This wasn't zen.

This was a zoo.

"Um? Mike? Ah…you know what? Suddenly, I'm not that hungry." Poppy stumbled over her words. She took one step back. Then two. "But maybe we could take a rain check?"

As much as she'd meant what she'd said only moments before, she didn't mean a word of what she was saying now. There was as much chance of her giving Mike a rain check as there was of a drought in Seattle.

"Sure…yeah…absolutely. It's supposed to rain next week."

Poppy disagreed. The forecast on any chance for romance with Mike was dry. High and dry.

She couldn't close the door behind her quickly enough. Poppy needed space—and a physical barrier—between her and Mike.

That whole idea she'd had earlier about listening to Megan? *Wrong.* How did this stuff always happen to her?

Adulting. Dating. Zen. *Pfft.* It was all for the birds. This day would go down in Poppy history as the worst ever. She shuffled her feet on the hardwood floor so that Megan would unquestionably know Poppy had returned and wasn't going back outside.

She wasn't returning to Mike—or to the dating pool at all. Ever.

"Ooh. You're back already. Two minutes. That is a record, even for you."

Poppy decided to lay down the truth. "I may not know what I want, but I know what I don't want."

The sound of gears shifting and tires squealing could be clearly heard out on the street.

"What was that?" Megan turned her head and looked toward the front door.

Poppy sat down on the tall stool at the counter

with a laugh. "That was the sound of the last time I let you fix me up."

"His ex said he was a catch."

"Maybe there's a reason she's his ex."

Megan didn't give in easily. "Or…maybe there's a reason you don't give anyone—or anything—a chance."

Poppy reached for the pitcher of water and poured herself a glass. After the last two-and-a-half minutes, she honestly could have used something stronger, but for now, water would have to do.

Besides, water could wash away that snippy tone in her sister's voice as well as anything could. "I give everything a chance."

Megan squinted her eyes, then glanced down as she transferred macaroni and cheese to a serving dish on the counter. "Really? How was the job at the dental office?"

"Not—"

"Not for you."

Poppy shrugged. She didn't like where this was going. "I don't like teeth."

"You know who that sounds like?" Megan lowered the boom.

Totally unfair. Her sister was not playing by the rules. Poppy wasn't going to take this lying down. She would sit up straight, here on this barstool, and defend herself.

"Don't say Mom."

"Did you read her last postcard?" Megan took a

small paper rectangle with a glossy photo of a bear on the front from the fridge and handed it to Megan. "She's in Maine on a hiking trip."

Gotcha, Poppy thought. She'd shut down this whole ridiculous comparison, stat. Megan didn't even know what was really going on with their mom right now. She'd correct her older sister and that would be the end of it.

"Oh! You're two weeks behind. I just saw on her Facebook page that she met a bunch of tourists, and she's joining them for a cruise."

"Exactly. She can't even commit to a hike."

Wait. Where did Megan pull that arrow from? Her sister's aim rang true. It pierced at Poppy's heart.

"Well I *can* commit," Poppy said, lowering her voice slightly. "I just haven't found the thing I'm really good at yet."

Megan wiped her hands on her apron. Poppy watched, feeling like Megan was wiping her hands clean of her flaky younger sister. The realization that she was twenty-eight and had no idea what she was good at—or what she should do with her life—hurt. She'd always been open to trying new things. But what if, instead of always being open to new ideas and new experiences, she should have been trying to buckle down and hone one particular craft or area of focus?

She'd always thought of her flexibility as a strength. Clearly, it had become a liability.

"Rob! Steve! Dinner's ready, okay?" Megan called

out to the boys, who were playing in the corner of the living room.

Suddenly, the small Craftsman house filled with the sound of little brother struggling with big brother. It reminded Poppy of more than a few arguments she and Megan had once had.

"Hey! No! It's my sword," Rob said.

Steve lunged at the toy. "Give it back."

"Ugh. The dragon again." Megan looked as *over it* as Poppy had felt when Mike had brought up his mother's size-two wedding dress. And the spring wedding. And the five kids.

So many options for why she dumped him. In fact, she could have used a fire-breathing dragon out there to drive home her point. Where were all the good dragons when you needed them? They were probably as fictional as the idea of a good man.

Poppy grabbed a roll of aluminum foil as a grin overtook her face. She might not know how to handle weird dates or weird jobs or other weird attempts at adulting, but swords, dragons, and elementary schoolers? No sweat. "I've got this."

"Thanks, Poppy."

"Hey guys, what's going on?"

"But Aunt Poppy…Steve won't give me his sword." Rob explained the situation with conviction. Life was tough when your little brother dogged your every move.

Steve didn't care about his brother's reasoning. "It's not my fault you broke yours."

Poppy paused, then looked around the room with an exaggerated manner. "Do you guys hear that?"

Instantly, the two boys paused. "Hear what?"

"It's the dragon. Breathing." Now that she had their attention, she improvised more of the story. "While you two fight over that sword, he's getting closer. Now, you know what's more important than a sword when you're defending yourself against a rogue dragon?"

They were hooked. Poppy threw herself into selling this scenario to the boys with all the gusto of an Oscar-worthy performance.

"No."

"A fireproof shield."

"Oh…" The boys were united in their understanding of what they needed to conquer the dragon.

Calm had come to the kingdom. Poppy wanted to pat herself on the back, but the battle was not yet over.

"Throw me that pillow." Poppy caught the blue square with one hand and began to wrap it in a length of tinfoil. "Now, if that dragon breathes on you, you are toast. You're worse than toast. You're *burnt* toast."

Both of her nephews stared, wide-eyed. She could feel their appreciation for her story. After all of today's craziness, it was a balm for her soul. Who knew that a fire-breathing dragon would be the best part of her day?

"Now go," Poppy spoke with conviction to the pint-sized knights. "Defeat the dragon. Both of you."

They took their orders seriously.

Steve held up the new shield atop their makeshift fort. "Ha. Take that. In your face, dragon!"

Rob brandished the sword. "We've gotcha now."

Poppy couldn't help but smile. Soon, the dragon would be slain. Too bad the utter mess her life seemed to have become couldn't be handled in the same way. She'd give anything to solve her current problems with a sword and some tinfoil.

She needed a knight in shining armor. But fairy tales weren't real. There was no knight riding into Seattle on a valiant steed named "Adulting," who was going to charge into her world and make everything work out.

Megan watched the scene with a smile as Poppy walked back across the open area between the living room and the kitchen. "Well, you do know I'm not getting that pillow back now, right?"

Poppy would take her victories where she found them.

"A small price to pay for saving the kingdom from ruin," she pointed out with a laugh in her voice. It felt good to shake off the day—and the idea that she needed her own hero. She could do this herself. She just had to figure out where her path led.

The boys ran toward the kitchen table with enthusiastic pride. "We did it!"

Steve high-fived his brother as they sat down. "We got him!"

"Yeah!" Poppy joined in their cheers. "That's awesome."

Megan caught Poppy's eye with a knowing nod. "This—" She gestured to the boys and their foil-covered weapons. "This is something you're really good at."

The boys immediately focused on dinner, as though everything in the house had instantly returned back to business as usual. "This broccoli is really good, mom," Rob said.

Steve echoed him with a simple sound of appreciation. "Mm-hmm."

But Poppy smiled, knowing her sister's words had changed everything. Maybe she could find her zen after all. Maybe all she needed was some time with children to turn her into a full-fledged adult.

Ryan Larson brushed off the knock at the door, followed by the sound of the doorbell. Whoever it was would just have to wait. It was probably just FedEx dropping off a package, anyway.

They could just leave it on the porch. He was on the phone with his lead developer who was on a business trip to Japan. This call from halfway around the world was one of the final keys to everything. It wouldn't be long until he was presenting to the entire Yamoharo Global team, persuading them to buy his new app technology.

Once they did, the sky would be the limit.

Until then, nothing in heaven or on earth could be a distraction. Especially not the doorbell.

"Look, we're getting five thousand downloads a day. And if we can land this, that number doubles. Yeah, I know. I hear what you're saying. Well, I don't think it's that complicated. We just tell them who we are, you know? We're a young, proven company. We've got apps that work. And this one has a great interface, it's simple…exactly."

Ryan paced across the front of his home office, oblivious to the light filtering through the windows or the sounds of the birds in the trees. He could feel it. One step closer to sealing the deal. "Yeah. And I just think we share the comments…I've got 'em right here."

Ryan dragged his finger across the touchpad mouse on his laptop and pulled up his email. He tapped the forward button and sent the summary brief with the feedback flying halfway around the world to the Land of the Rising Sun.

Suddenly he couldn't keep his focus anymore. A woman in a lightweight brown jacket was jumping up and down and waving and flailing outside the window to his office. He lived in a popular neighborhood with lots of families and hustle and bustle. But a strange woman dressed in fall-appropriate layers and practically tap-dancing in his front yard was something he'd never seen before. "I've got to call you back."

His colleague acknowledged receipt of the email. Ryan wrapped up the conversation. Through the window, he gestured for the woman to meet him at the front door.

Ryan opened the dark wooden door and a woman with loose brown curls and a pearly smile stood just in front of him.

"Can I help you?" he asked. He needed to get this over with so he could make a few more phone calls before the time difference between Seattle and Japan made it difficult to continue any of the day's discussions. Sometimes, it seemed hard to work globally—especially without Laurie. He'd been able to work all day and all night before she got sick. Laurie ran the house, Ryan ran the business.

Together, they helped each other achieve their dreams. It had been the ideal partnership, and although it had been nearly four years since ovarian cancer stole her from the family they'd created together, he still felt a twinge of regret when he thought of what was missing from his life and the kids' lives. Some days, it felt very lonely without a wife and mother to keep all the balls in the air and to fill the four walls around them with love.

"Oh, I'm Poppy Summerall. Temporarily for You—I made a business card and everything."

She handed him a business card that looked like she'd made it on her home computer. It declared the name of her business to be *Temporarily for You Nanny Services*. There were clouds dotting the background of the card. He'd never seen anything quite like it.

But at least he now knew who the crazy dancing lady in the front yard was. He'd gotten so caught up in the call that he'd forgotten she was supposed to come by today. "Yes, you're Megan's sister."

Megan had become a friend over the years. Their kids played together. Megan had brought Zoe and Zach home from school in a pinch when one nanny or another quit or Ryan needed to work late. She dished out practical, thoughtful mom advice without making him feel like a clueless dad.

Ryan trusted Megan. So, when she said that her sister Poppy would be perfect to take care of the kids, Ryan believed her.

"And you're Ryan Larson," Poppy said.

If he'd been oblivious to everything this afternoon except conversations with techie types, he wasn't now. Poppy had an easy smile and a twinkle in her blue eyes.

She looked like someone the kids could warm up to. Eventually. Poor lady probably didn't even know what she was in for. The kids had taken all of their recent nannies by surprise.

And there had been a string of them lately.

He took a deep breath and nodded, opening the door wide for her to enter. "Yeah, come on in."

"Thank you."

"Did you have any trouble finding the place?"

"No. I just looked for the only house on the block without Halloween decorations."

Her observation brought back more memories of Laurie. Ryan had been so caught up in the presentation he needed to make in a few weeks that he'd put off everything having to do with the upcoming holiday. And now it was basically too late. Laurie never would have let that happen. Laurie had a way of making every holiday special.

"Yeah…yeah…Halloween was kind of my wife's thing." Ryan hoped the new nanny couldn't hear the regret in his voice. He didn't want to start off on the wrong foot with this one. Goodness knows there had been enough wrong feet with the wrong nannies around here for a while.

"Oh, I'm sorry. I didn't mean to…" Poppy apologized.

Ryan hadn't intended for her to feel badly about his observation. He needed to change the conversation quickly and keep this moving forward. "No, no… It's okay. It's been almost four years now." Ryan needed this nanny to work out. "Anyway…thank you for coming. My company is expanding one of our apps. It's crunch time."

"I can crunch!" Her voice squeaked up a few octaves. She reminded Ryan of a cheerleader on the sidelines of a college football game.

"Great—great." Poppy's enthusiasm set him at ease. There was just one more hurdle to clear. But it was the big one. "Well, let me introduce you."

"Okay."

Ryan walked to the base of the stairs and shouted upward at the kids. "Hey, guys—come and meet Poppy."

"Do we have to?" Zoe's skepticism echoed from the second floor.

"She's your new nanny, so, yes." Ryan's jaw clenched. Why was his daughter being difficult?

Zoe's stubborn streak didn't go away. "We don't want a new nanny."

"Tell them I'm a mermaid," Poppy whispered, leaning close to Ryan's ear.

He caught a slight whiff of her perfume. He thought it might have been patchouli—which seemed fitting for someone named Poppy.

It felt ridiculous to tell the kids that their new nanny was a mythical creature. They were way too smart to believe that. But he didn't have any better options, so he went with it as the kids stepped down to the staircase. "She's a mermaid."

After a pause that felt like it could be measured in years, not seconds, the kids came down the stairs. Zoe's low, dark pigtails gave a defiant bounce as she screeched to a halt at the landing. Zach just barely cleared his older sister's shoulder. He kept everything but his mop of blond hair tucked behind it, as though Zoe was not just a sibling, but a defensive fort.

"Hi." Poppy stayed just behind Ryan as she gave a half-wave.

Zoe rolled her eyes. If Ryan didn't know better, he'd swear his eleven-year-old fifth-grader had fully morphed into the junior high years right before his eyes. "I told you she's not a real mermaid."

"Ah, that's Zoe."

"Hi, Zoe." The chipper sound of Poppy's voice belied any inner turmoil she might have reasonably had after the first impression Zoe just dished out.

"Hello." His little teen-in-training now sounded as flat as a puddle.

"And the boy hiding behind his big sister is Zach." Ryan tried to read his son's face, but it remained emotionless. Only the quirk at the far end of the left eyebrow betrayed his carefully stoic appearance.

Zach leaned over to Zoe as she whispered something behind a cupped hand. In spite of the cold shoulder she had to be feeling from the kids, Poppy forged ahead with the pleasantries.

"Hello, Zach. You know, I've got a big sister, too. Her kids go to your school."

Without another word, the kids ran back up the stairs. Their behavior embarrassed Ryan. He knew they were just kids and that things had been awkward for so long. First, they'd lost their mother, and ever since, there'd been a constant stream of nannies. Poppy was just another face in a long line of temporary help brought in to manage the chaos.

But Poppy didn't know that, and he feared that the bright woman with the eager grin and shoulder-length curls would start to plot how soon she could make an exit.

And when she did, that would upend everything. With the Yamoharo Global presentation coming up, he didn't have time to find another nanny. He barely had time to make the introductions for this one.

Maybe if he laughed off their sullen reactions, she'd laugh them off too. "Ha ha. Sorry. They'll warm right up to you."

"That's okay. They must have really liked their last nanny."

"Oh, that's a long story…" Bless her for thinking it was that simple. Fortunately, Ryan's phone rang before he had a chance to dig *that* hole and dive face-first into it. Poppy did not need to know the truth of Zach and Zoe's feelings about Barbara Lewis, the last nanny. He still remained grateful that the 911 dispatcher on duty that evening had a sense of humor. The nanny didn't, but under the circumstances, that was understandable.

He saw the call was from Jean, his assistant. Ryan didn't even have to hear any of her words to know he was going to be late for his next meeting. "I'm on my way."

Ryan didn't really want to just throw Poppy to the wolves—*kids*, he corrected himself—but nannying was her job. And he had more than enough of his own job to worry about at this moment. Surely, Poppy would be fine with the kids. They just needed to get used to her. He slid his phone into his left pocket. "Okay, we good to go?"

"Yeah. All nannied up!" Once again, Poppy reminded him of a cheerleader. Maybe this would be okay. His kids needed some cheer in their lives.

Honestly, it would have to be okay. He didn't have any time between now and the presentation at the end of the month to solve another nanny or child crisis.

He just needed to get to the office, hope for the best, and let Poppy and the kids sort out Poppy-and-the-kids kinds of things.

"Great. I don't usually work Sundays but this is a crazy week, so…" Ryan opened the hall closet and grabbed out his briefcase and a light jacket. "Emergency numbers are on the fridge. Here are these…" He handed Poppy a set of house keys and a credit card to use for activities.

Then, he looked around and lowered his voice. He might be leaving the Poppy-and-the-kids kinds of things to Poppy and the kids, but he did know one covert weapon that would definitely help Poppy in the process. "And the secret password is 'pumpkinhead'… for now."

"Got it," Poppy said, with an obviously false confidence which confirmed to his ears that she had no idea what he was talking about. It didn't matter— he had to go. He'd just have to let her figure it out.

"Have a good one." Ryan hoped that his sentiment wasn't just a false hope.

She took off her jacket and tossed it over the top of the newel post. "Yeah, you too."

"Thanks." Ryan took off for the front door before the kids could realize he was leaving. Once again, his phone started to ring. He reached in his pocket and started to answer out of habit without even thinking about who was on the other end of the line or what he was saying. "Hello…yes, this is—"

He just needed to make it to the end of the month. Right now, everything was a blur.

Well, everything except the twinkle in Poppy Summerall's blue eyes when she smiled.

Ryan could see that in his mind's eye very clearly.

Chapter Two

THE KIDS MAY NOT HAVE taken to her, but Poppy was committed. Well, at least temporarily.

However, in order to make it through the next month, Poppy knew she'd have to get the kids on her side. She thought of the rough-and-tumble fun she'd had with her nephews while she'd been staying with them. If she could just get through to Zoe and Zach, there would be fun in the Larson house, too.

As Poppy walked up the stairs, her eyes locked on a smiling family portrait framed and hanging on the wall. She clearly recognized Ryan and the kids in the frame—although the kids were much younger. Zach looked barely old enough to qualify for toddlerhood. He sat on the lap of a woman with shoulder-length blonde hair. That must have been Ryan's wife.

Sadness tugged at Poppy's heart. Sadness for the woman who wouldn't get to see her kids grow up. Sadness for the man who wouldn't get to grow old with the woman he'd married. Sadness for the kids who would only know their mother through stories.

None of those emotions surprised her.

But what did surprise her was the last fleeting twist of those emotions that whispered to her, *You'd better figure out this commitment thing for real, Poppy, or you'll never have anything like this...*

Poppy had spent her whole adult life drifting from one idea to another, like a balloon.

A human balloon, that's what she'd been. But not anymore. She was committed. These kids needed her. They needed fun stories of their own to tell about growing up. Poppy felt like she owed it to the woman in the picture frame to see to it that her kids were happy in the time that they were in Poppy's care.

She couldn't bring their mother back, but she could commit to Zoe and Zach that she would help them enjoy their time together and would do her best while she worked here.

Poppy paused at the door across the landing from the stairs. Pink, sparkly letters had been affixed to the white paint declaring "Zoe's Room." A sign just below gave further instruction.

"No boys allowed by order of Zoe." Poppy smiled. She remembered the "boys have cooties" years.

One more sign further clarified the situation: a rectangle of purple construction paper with glittery heart-shaped stickers attached declared "Except Zach sometimes."

It was good to see that Zoe seemed to have a strong friendship with her brother.

Poppy knocked briefly on the door. "You guys in there?"

"Yes."

"Noooo."

The responses from inside Zoe's room contradicted each other.

"Ouch. I mean no." Apparently the primary occupant of the room had quickly applied some tough-love diplomacy to her little brother.

Brothers and sisters were the same everywhere. "Can I come in?" Poppy asked with a laugh she couldn't contain.

"What's the password?" Zoe's voice sounded muffled behind the door.

Poppy decided to play this one out for a bit. "Password."

"Not even close," Zoe scolded.

"Flibbertigibbet." Poppy threw out the silliest word she could think of.

"No." Zoe sounded exasperated.

"Bingo-bongo."

"No." This time, it was Zach's turn to yell.

"I don't...um..." Now was the time. "Pumpkinhead?"

The door opened wide. Zach stared in silent disbelief. Zoe leaned against the door she'd just opened and crossed her arms. A scowl fixed heavily across her face.

"My dad told you," the young girl said accusingly. Even the dark brown pigtails that fell on either side of her face seemed to be throwing some serious shade in Poppy's direction.

Poppy raised her eyebrows. She didn't really want to shove her new boss completely under the bus. "Maybe." Racking her brain, she tried to think of a reason for her to know the password other than learning it from Ryan. "Or maybe mermaids can read minds."

Zach threw a glance at his sister. He was torn between believing Poppy's magical answer and remaining loyal to his sister.

Play it cool, Poppy, she reminded herself. If she could get Zach to buy the mermaid logic, maybe she could get Zoe to suspend her disbelief too.

"What am I thinking?" Zoe wasn't quite prepared to let Poppy off the hook.

"Hmmm…you're thinking…*what am I thinking?*" Poppy figured it would be a no-brainer to throw Zoe's own words back at her, because naturally, she had to have thought the words first in order to have said them.

Before either kid could have a chance to respond, Poppy changed the subject.

"You guys want to go have some fun?" she asked.

Much to Poppy's relief, the kids nodded slowly, eyes still wide with the last, lingering traces of skepticism. If she could just come up with the right thing to do, Poppy thought she might begin to win Zoe and Zach over.

Fun seemed to be a universal language—no password needed.

Sundays in the fall were made for playing catch with your kids and picking apples, not glass walls and polished bamboo floors, Ryan thought as he walked down the hallway toward his office.

Everything surrounding him looked perfect. A black server cabinet stood off to his left in a separate, glass-enclosed room. The lights on the front of the big metal box blinked slowly at him, each blue dot making Ryan feel colder and more alone.

He shook off the guilty feeling that had settled on his shoulders. It was a sacrifice to give up his weekend with the kids to be here at the office, but in the end, it would be worth it. If the sale to Yamoharo Global went through without a hitch, it would benefit the kids. College without loans, trips to Disney World—pretty much everything for Zach and Zoe's future—both practical and fun—would be within Ryan's reach.

If he could stay focused for the next month and cross the finish line.

He just had to stay the course. That's why he'd brought Poppy into their lives.

He sat down at his desk and flipped open the sleek gray laptop. The background of the computer flashed the Parcel Technologies green and yellow and blue knot-style logo. Every time he saw it, it brought him a feeling of contented pride. He'd promised Laurie he'd take care of the kids. And here was the proof. Parcel Technologies—their dream to secure their future—was thriving. By the end of the month, the company would be going places and partnering with global powerhouses. Neither he nor Laurie could have ever dreamed about such a thing during their heart-to-heart talks as the cancer pulled her further and further away from her family.

He clicked the envelope icon and brought up his inbox, intending to clear out whatever was in there first before he started the in-office part of his day.

The screen lit up yellow with row after row of brand-new emails. Most of them were from the advisor he'd hired to guide him through the intricacies of working with a Japanese company. Abigail Morwell spoke fluent Japanese and had been a highly-sought-after consultant to several other Pacific Northwest tech start-ups who were selling their apps to conglomerates in Asia.

She knew her stuff, but Ryan was convinced she never slept—or thought about anything other than the deal at hand.

A pop-up message quickly assessed the level of damage: *Welcome, Ryan. You have 450 new messages.*

All he could do was laugh. He was going to be at the office far longer than he'd planned today.

"That's got to be a new inbox record," he said out loud—even though he was the only one there to hear it.

The Whidbey Island Harvest Festival was one of the landmark events signaling fall had come to the Pacific Northwest. Ever since she'd visited with her nephews for the first time several years ago, Poppy had sworn she'd never miss this annual fun.

Signs at the entrance pointed the way to "Corn Huskin'" and "Candy Apple Lane" and "Jack-O'-Lantern Junction." Poppy took in a deep breath of the fall air. It felt as crisp as one of the bright red apples that would be used for apple bobbing.

Poppy had second-guessed a lot about her life lately, but bringing the Larson kids here definitely felt like she'd made the right decision. There was no way they could keep their pouting faces on here. Balloons, hay bales, pumpkins…what here *couldn't* put a smile on any face?

"Now *this* is a harvest festival." Poppy strolled past the mini Ferris wheel with one little Larson on either side.

Zoe still refused to give up her interrogation. "If you're a mermaid, then where's your tail?"

Poppy decided the best way to beat the precocious girl at her own game was to play along instead of fighting against the stream of questions. "It only comes out in the ocean."

"What do you eat?" Zoe would not be deterred.

"Seaweed and algae." That seemed like a reasonable answer to Poppy, although she picked up a bag of popcorn off a red picnic table as she answered. She proceeded to toss a few fluffy kernels in her mouth, despite the fact that popcorn wasn't on the approved list of mermaid foods.

"You don't eat fish?" Zoe grabbed her own bag of popcorn, then handed another small striped sack to her brother.

Spinning the story started to become second nature to Poppy. She fired off the answer rapidly. "No...fish are my friends."

"Do you speak fish?"

"Fluently. But my French is better." *Got her.* Zoe stayed several steps behind, overcome by silence. Zach followed Poppy as she strode purposefully toward freshly-shucked corn piled high atop a red-and-white checkerboard tablecloth. It all seemed so...harvesty. Poppy loved it. And she was ready to move on from the relentless barrage of questions and start enjoying this perfect afternoon with the kids.

"Corn on the cob," Poppy said to Zach. "Do you know how to pick out corn?"

He shook his head.

Poppy placed both of their popcorn bags at the edge of the picnic table, then began to dig in the pile of yellow and green in front of them. "So, get the ones that are, like, kind of yellow underneath. Those are the good ones."

Zoe ran up behind Poppy and forced herself in the space next to her brother. This time, she adopted the rapid-fire approach. "What's your favorite food? How many marshmallows can you fit in your mouth at one time? What's the scariest rollercoaster you've ever been on? And can ghosts swim?"

Poppy returned fire with a seriousness that she hoped would let Zoe know she was taking the motive behind the girl's questions seriously. She knew Zoe was feeling the new nanny out in her own youthful way, and Poppy respected that. "Anything with mustard. Nine. Drop of Doom. Only fish ghosts."

Finally, Zoe laughed. "What are we going to do with all this corn?"

The change of subject brought a smile to Poppy's face. "We're going to make cornbread."

"Yeah, what are we going to do with that?" This time, Zoe's question was genuine.

"We're going to eat it—along with the chili we're going to make for dinner. Does your dad like chili?" A frown wrinkled Poppy's face. This grand dinner plan had come to her while strolling across the Harvest Festival, but she'd completely disregarded the fact that she didn't know any of the Larson family's likes or dislikes when it came to food.

"He eats at work." Zoe's shoulders slumped and she picked at the silk threads on an ear of corn. "That's why you're with us. So he doesn't have to be."

Poppy tried to reassure her. "I bet he wishes he was here."

"I hate cornbread." Zoe's whole demeanor had changed from just seconds before.

Clearly, Zoe was going to be a challenge. One

minute, Poppy thought she'd finally broken through. The next minute, the girl had fallen back into her old, defensive, skeptical habits. Poppy had to find a way to get through to her. But how?

"More for me!" Zach announced. Poppy wished Zoe's resistance could be broken down as quickly as Zach's. The younger Larson had already started to warm to Poppy, and Poppy loved it. She remembered when her own family split up and how she'd wished for a grown-up who understood and tried to make things better.

Poppy wanted to be that grown-up for these kids. They deserved some stability in their lives and someone who would be there during more than just the hours when they were asleep.

"And meeee." She raised her hand and gave Zach a high-five. He enthusiastically slapped Poppy's hand back.

There, Poppy thought with a smile. They were officially on the same team. Hashtag: Nanny Goals.

This felt good.

Until two seconds later, when Zach began to scream. "SPIDER! Spider! Spider!" He ran off, still screaming. "Aaugh!"

"Let's go." Poppy dropped her armful of corn ears back atop the pile on the table and began to run toward the barn, in pursuit of Zach.

"Zach? Where are you going?" Zoe's attitude of distrust immediately dropped. She sprinted ahead as though nothing mattered more than her brother.

Poppy followed quickly behind. "Zach?"

Zoe continued yelling after her brother as she rounded picnic tables and zigzagged between other festival-goers enjoying a lazy Sunday stroll through the grounds. "Zach!"

Finally, they caught up to him near the goat stall. Zach sat sullenly on a bench. The colorful pumpkins and flowers on the table behind him sat in cheerful contrast to his visible turmoil. Poppy squatted down to be at eye level with him as she tried to offer reassurance.

"Hmm…so I think spiders might like corn on the cob as much as people do. Sorry, buddy."

A small shard of guilt tore at her heart. He'd only started picking through the ears of corn because Poppy had. She needed to make it right. But she could see in Zach's gray eyes that he was desperately trying to sort out his own emotions.

Poppy wanted to honor his desire to be a big kid, to find his place in a world where he hadn't had much control over the larger events. In her soul, she felt like she needed to just punch the pause button and give Zach some space.

She pointed at the fenced-in goat pen just a few steps away. Zoe was kneeling in front of the gate, petting one of the animals inside. "Okay, I'm going to be right over there, if you need me—" Poppy patted him on the knee and then pointed a thumb over her shoulder. "Right there."

Poppy strolled over to the goat pen and leaned on

the green metal bars of the gate. "Hey, Zoe." Maybe while Zach was sorting out his fear of arachnids, she and Zoe could sort out the young girl's skepticism of the new nanny.

"Let me guess. He's not talking to you." Zoe summed up the situation pretty succinctly. Poppy assumed Zoe had seen this reaction before.

"Nope. That's okay. Talking's overrated." Poppy threw a quick glance over her shoulder to check on Zach, then turned back and waved her fingers at the half-dozen goats walking around the pen and bleating. "I'm going to talk to these guys. Hey, nanny. Hi, I'm a nanny too."

Zoe followed the train of thought. "I know why they call it a nanny goat."

"Why?"

"Because nannies come in and try to take over."

Ouch. Zoe's truth bomb just explained everything about her reluctant attitude since she'd first been summoned to the stairs at the house to meet Poppy.

Another shriek from another Larson child broke through the general sounds of joy at the Harvest Festival. This time, it was Zoe. "My favorite sweater!"

Poppy looked down. Three goats had crowded up to Zoe and were pulling her knitted sweater through the bars of the pen's gate. Poppy clearly heard the sound of fabric ripping as the lead goat took the hem in her teeth and stepped back, tearing a hole in Zoe's garment.

A fear of spiders, Poppy could deal with. But

fending off goats was a whole different thing. This was a nanny curveball she never could have imagined. The Whidbey Island Harvest Festival had attack goats.

Think fast, Poppy... "Okay—okay... Off! Roll over! Spit! Heel!"

The goats followed nanny directives just about as well as the Larson kids did.

Finally, Zoe disengaged. She looked down at what remained of the hem of her sweater and waggled it at Poppy. Then she narrowed her eyes and leaned toward Poppy defensively. "This is all your fault! I want to go home."

"Me too." Zach finally broke his silence.

"Me three." Poppy surrendered.

Somehow, she made it through dinner without engendering too much conflict. The kids mostly kept to themselves. They picked at their chili and homemade cornbread, but Poppy was too drained to encourage them to eat any better. Today hadn't gone quite as planned.

Okay, it hadn't gone *at all* as planned.

When Megan told Poppy she was good at taking care of kids, Poppy thought that had to mean something. If an unbiased third-party saw something capable in her, that had to count, right?

Yet, just like tossing pizza dough, bonding with kids was harder than it looked. It was time to confront the fact that her nephews probably liked her simply because she was their aunt. They were related. The boys had to like her.

Total strangers…that was another story entirely.

And one that would not have a happy ending, Poppy feared.

After dinner, she tried a string of activities to get the kids engaged, but nothing worked. Everything just got tossed aside after no more than a few minutes into a big, colorful mess of failures. Once the kids had been in bed for about an hour, Poppy ventured back upstairs to check on them. At least maybe she could dare to hope that they'd like her in their dreams. Poppy tiptoed into Zach's room. He was soundly sleeping, a fact which relieved Poppy greatly. Hopefully he wouldn't see any spiders while his eyes were closed.

She shuffled down the hallway to Zoe's room. The door stood open. Poppy leaned in around the doorway. A twitch under the covers tipped Poppy off. Zoe was faking sleep.

Zoe had to know Poppy was there. May as well acknowledge it. Poppy held her breath in a little bit of hesitation, fearing what else Zoe might have been thinking up to say as she tossed and turned. "Sleep well," Poppy said softly. She figured that was a benign, but caring, sentiment. Hopefully it wouldn't backfire on her and turn into another war of words.

"You woke me," Zoe said accusingly as she flopped onto her back.

"Awesome." She ran her hands through her hair and thought back to yoga stretches and pizza dough and size two wedding dresses. She shook her head. She wasn't going to find her zen nannying either.

This was one more commitment that wasn't going to go the distance.

Pulling into the driveway after a long day of answering hundreds of emails and participating in conference calls, Ryan couldn't believe how late it was. The Seattle sky wasn't just dark, it looked pitch black. The time had gotten far, far away from him. He hadn't meant to leave Poppy with the kids this long on their first day together, it was just…

As he got out of the car, Ryan reminded himself to keep his focus. It was just…temporary. That was the word he was looking for. Temporary. Soon, all the craziness surrounding the presentation to Yamoharo Global would be in the past and the future for the entire Larson family would be sunny and bright.

He walked in the house quietly, knowing the kids had to have been asleep for hours.

Blankets and a feather boa were strewn over the staircase rail. In the entryway, Ryan gingerly stepped over a jump rope and something else that he couldn't exactly identify, best described as doughy. A bomb might as well have gone off in his house while he'd been away. He didn't know whether to call 911 or just be glad that the kids seemed to have made good use of all the toys he'd bought them.

Poppy sat on the dining room rug, blotting up something with a blue towel.

"Don't worry…it's just a little bit of blood."

"Ah…" Yup, he should have just called 911.

"I'm kidding. It's just juice."

The laugh Poppy gave seemed just a little too enthusiastic.

"So, things went well then?" He couldn't quite tell what the true state of affairs actually was.

Poppy's wide grin never wavered. "Completely painless."

"Don't worry about the rug. Please. The kids asleep?" Ryan took off his jacket and laid it over a chair. One more thing out of place wasn't going to make much difference.

"One is. The other's faking." Poppy stood up and tossed the towel from one hand to the other as she walked. "I took them to the Harvest Festival, where Zach had an unfortunate arachnid incident, and Zoe's favorite sweater is currently being digested by a goat."

The lift of her eyebrow finally gave it away. She was exhausted and overwhelmed.

"Oh…" Ryan understood both of those feelings at the moment. His day had been exactly the same. The only difference was that the chaos had been caused by computers, not children.

"They are…wonderful kids." She dropped her voice and the tone became serious.

He knew where this was headed. He'd heard it before. Last week, to be exact. And two months before that. And three weeks before that. "Oh no."

"Funny—and unique—and engaging…"

Poppy continued the litany of attributes. Ryan

knew they were only justifications for the explosive device she was about to toss at his feet.

"Oh no…" The sound that came out of his mouth sounded more like a growl. He recognized it as the bellow of a wounded animal. He'd heard it on National Geographic before—he just never assumed he would hear it in his own kitchen, coming from his own throat. "You're quitting."

"I just don't think this is for me." At least she had the grace to sound remorseful about it.

This would go down in the record books as the fastest hire-to-quit time frame for any of the nannies he'd hired. "It's only been one day."

"Is that all?" The circles under her eyes confirmed what he already knew about the events she'd put up with today. Ryan studied her face. The perfect brown waves her hair had been curled into this morning now drooped like water at low tide. Poppy seemed drained of all the optimism and energy she'd shown this morning when she'd bounced onto his doorstep with her homemade business card.

"Okay, a long day…but, you know…" Ryan searched for the right words to reassure her, to make her see that in time, things would be better.

He could not lose another nanny. As he'd told Poppy earlier, it was crunch time. He could not afford any more lack of focus. Yamoharo Global would not understand if the presentation in a few weeks' time did not check every box, answer every question, and overcome every possible objection.

His company's future depended upon it.

His kids' future depended upon it—even though they didn't understand that now.

Everything depended on Poppy and keeping her here to look after the kids so he could focus a few weeks of time exclusively on what stood just around the corner.

"The truth is—" Poppy looked around the room covertly as she rolled her eyes slightly and dropped her voice to a whisper. "I'm not actually a nanny."

"I know."

"I've never done this before—except with my sister's kids—and they have to be nice to me, because we're related." She paused for breath and then looked right at Ryan. Her eyes went wide as she searched his face, seemingly looking for a sign of surprise. "Wait… what?"

She'd been honest with him. Now it was Ryan's turn to be honest with Poppy. Maybe if they built a foundation of truth between each other, they could make this work. He was always telling the kids that honesty was the best policy. Maybe it worked for nannies too. "Your sister told me on the phone the other day."

"And you still hired me? You must be really desperate."

"No, it's just…" Ryan didn't want to admit how truthful her observation was. He *was* desperate. Completely. And they both knew it. "Please…can you just hang on a couple more weeks?"

She picked up juice boxes and disposed of them. "You don't have any relatives?"

"Well, sure we have relatives. We're not *those* people," he said with a chuckle, trying to lighten the mood. It didn't work. Poppy continued methodically picking up kid trash and throwing it away. Ryan picked up two wadded-up napkins and took them to the trash can. "Just no relatives around here."

She paused. Maybe he would survive until the end of the month after all.

"What day is today?" Poppy ran one hand on either side of her head, threading through her thick, naturally-highlighted hair.

"Still Sunday." How was that even possible? There was no way this was the same bright and sunny day it had been when he'd walked out the door earlier.

She shook her head dejectedly. "Yeah, that's what I thought."

"Look, I get it. Kids are a huge commitment. Even when they're not yours."

Poppy's head snapped up with precise attention. Her back straightened and her shoulders pushed back. Ryan watched the subtle movements completely transform her features and her body language in just a matter of seconds.

"I can commit. I can commit. Until the end of the month."

"What about...next month—Thanksgiving?" *Hey...if they were bargaining...might as well shoot for the moon.*

45

"This month—Halloween."

He knew this was as good as he would get out of Poppy Summerall. He'd take it and be thankful. "Perfect. Deal. Great. Thank you."

"I'll see you tomorrow." She sounded resigned to the fact. But she'd just confirmed she'd be back here at the house, and that's all that mattered to Ryan right now.

"Say, do you think you could do, like, six a.m.?"

"Don't push it. But I'm committing." She gave a little fist-bump motion as she pivoted and headed for the front of the house before the conversation could go any further. She swiftly dodged the toys scattered everywhere as she got away.

Ryan felt the dryness in his throat abate.

"Committing," Poppy reiterated, then disappeared out the door.

Ryan walked into the kitchen. He had to clean up a huge mess tonight. But at least he didn't have to deal with the added mess of sourcing another nanny.

Poppy had declared she was committed to the job.

Ryan knew he was committed to getting through the Yamoharo Global presentation.

Now, if he could just get the kids to commit to the idea that Poppy was there to help them all.

Through the windows that framed the entire back wall of Megan's house, Poppy could see the glow from the firepit in the backyard. Her sister sat in an Adirondack chair, drinking a mug of tea. A string of fairy lights twinkled off to one side.

In short, the entire scene looked idyllic, and idyllic was exactly what Poppy needed after the longest Sunday in the history of Sundays.

If Poppy were to find her zen anywhere in Seattle, Megan's back patio could be where it was hiding.

"Hello, Sister." Poppy greeted Megan formally. After all, she'd been the one who had looped Poppy into this whole mess of insanity.

Megan bobbed the tea bag in her mug and tucked a lock of stick-straight black hair behind one ear. "How did it go?"

"Don't ask." Poppy sat down and leaned back in the chair. Like all Adirondack chairs, there was no cushion to sink into, but Poppy wasn't sure she'd ever been more comfortable. It felt good to just sit and let her guard down.

"Just tell me you didn't quit already."

If only Megan knew how close she'd come. "I didn't quit."

"But you're going to." Her dark brown eyes fixed squarely on Poppy's face.

Poppy could tell Megan had already resigned herself to the inevitable answer.

Under normal circumstances, she would have taken great pleasure in giving her big sister the exact opposite response from what she was clearly expecting. But tonight, she felt too tired to play games. A bone-deep weariness had settled in every cell in her body, and the feeling came out even in her voice. "I told him I would stay until Halloween."

"He's a good guy." Megan leaned back in her chair and delivered the pronouncement with a dash of smug. Even the silver zipper on her blue jacket winked at Poppy as it reflected the glow of the moon above.

Maybe they were discussing two different Ryan Larsons. Poppy gave her sister a dose of side-eye. "He's a workaholic."

"And he's cute."

Megan hadn't lost the all-knowing tone of voice.

"If you like geek-chic." Poppy tried to throw Megan off this line of questioning.

"And you do," she answered, before taking another sip from the mug.

What was that supposed to even mean in the greater scheme of things?

"He's my boss." Megan knew about Poppy's dating rules…even if they were more often used as a defense mechanism or a good, old-fashioned excuse.

"Temporarily," Megan emphasized with a teasing smile. "Come on. How am I supposed to live vicariously through my single sister's dating life if you don't have a dating life?"

Her sister had been married too long and her brother-in-law had been on a ship too long. The Navy needed to bring Gary home, stat, so her sister could have her own love life without worrying about Poppy's—or the obvious lack thereof.

Poppy zipped her jacket halfway against the deep evening fall chill. "Any word from Gary?"

"We Skyped this morning. I can't wait until he's back." Megan's smile made Poppy want to blush. Not everyone had a love like her sister and brother-in-law had found.

"And I'm not leaving until he is." The sentiment was said to make Megan feel more secure, but it spoke to Poppy at a deeper level. She loved it here in Seattle, and it wasn't just about being close to her nephews.

"Thanks, Poppy. The house feels a lot less empty with you here. The kids and I couldn't do without you."

Time to get the conversation back on track. Since Megan seemed to have all the answers tonight, maybe she'd know what to do about the bigger problem. "So, what are we going to do about the fact that Ryan's kids don't want me there?"

Megan took a sip of her tea and then gave her advice with a wave of her hand. "Just be you."

Poppy sighed heavily. Megan made it seem so easy. Magical, even. But there was no fairy wand to fix Zoe's mistrust or Zach's skepticism. She had been herself today. She'd taken them to one of her favorite places, the Harvest Festival. She'd tried to cook them a special dinner. She'd planned for them to prepare it together, with farm-fresh ingredients.

All the effort that had gone into her first—and very long—day with the Larson kids had come from somewhere deep inside Poppy.

And still, just being her hadn't been good enough.

"Zach, I didn't do anything," Zoe squealed down the hall.

Weren't they supposed to be asleep?

It had to be after midnight. Ryan checked the time at the top of the electronic tablet in his hand. A whirlwind of chaos was thundering toward the master bedroom. So much for finishing up a few things before he turned out the lights himself.

"Yes, you did." Whatever Zoe's side of the story was, her brother didn't believe a word of it.

Zoe reiterated her innocence. "No, I didn't."

"Dad!" Zach rushed toward the bed in his too-small blue T-shirt and gray flannel camo-patterned pajama pants.

Ryan briefly looked up, but kept tapping on the tablet's touchscreen keyboard. "What's the matter, buddy? Can't sleep?"

"Zoe put a spider in my bed." Zach's dark blonde hair had been shocked into a serious case of bedhead.

Zoe ran in to defend herself. "Hey, that's not what I said. I said, *what if I did?*"

"You said you'd put it in my bed." Zach sounded close to tears, and that wasn't going to help anyone get a good night's sleep.

"No, I said *maybe I might.*" Zoe refused to give an inch. The hand on her hip seemed to match perfectly with her hot-pink-and-white polka-dot pajamas.

How could pajamas enhance sass? Ryan felt a chill go through him as he once again considered the upcoming teenage years.

But more than that, Ryan wondered how this fight had even gotten started in the first place. Poppy indicated the kids had both gone to bed hours ago. "Guys, come on, come on. Come up here."

Zach crawled up on the bed.

It reminded Ryan of when the kids were babies and they'd fall asleep on his chest. He missed those days and felt it deep in his heart. "Okay, there are absolutely no spiders—"

Zoe said, "Dad, Mrs. Brower said we all eat eight spiders in our sleep every year."

What were they teaching in school these days?

Zach snuggled up closer, practically wrapping himself in a ball. Ryan hadn't seen him lose it this much over a spider in months. "I don't wanna eat a spider. I hate spiders. I don't want to go to bed."

"I'm sorry, Dad," Zoe said. "I'm just saying what I heard. It's a fact."

"Thank you. Go to bed."

Zoe sighed and rolled her eyes, clearly bothered by the fact that no one appreciated her scientific wisdom. But at least she went back to bed the first time he asked her to. Ryan decided to give thanks for small miracles.

He tucked Zach in the crook of his arm and gave his boy a kiss on the head as they both leaned back against the bank of steel-gray pillows piled high against the dark mahogany headboard. Why couldn't anything be easy right now?

The school might be teaching Zoe some crazy things, but Ryan was the one who felt like he was failing.

Chapter Three

POPPY STOPPED ON THE LARSONS' front step to collect her thoughts.

Committed.

She could do this.

She *needed* to do this.

She needed to prove to Megan—and to herself—that she had it in her. Whatever *it* actually was.

Poppy turned her key in the lock and opened the door, then heard exactly what she'd expected to hear—Ryan Larson, the workaholic-in-chief, on a business call.

"Yeah, that's the big final…" he paused briefly, listening to the other person on the line. "All right, see what you can do and get back to me. Hey, and tell Higashimoto how excited we are. I've gotta run. My breakfast meeting is here. Bye."

Ryan disconnected the call, narrowly missing wiping a swipe of peanut butter on his prized smartphone.

"Breakfast meeting, huh?" At least that sounded

like he had time made in his schedule for her—even if it did sound like her presence in the house was just another box to check, another cog in the wheel.

"Ah—I wasn't sure you were going to make it." He laid his phone down on the counter, an action which shocked Poppy a bit. She didn't think she'd seen him before without it attached to his hand.

"Temporarily for You," she said, reminding herself almost as much as him. "Plus, I said I would."

"Coffee?"

Japanese business transactions were completely foreign to Poppy. But this—coffee—now Ryan was speaking her language.

"Sure. Cream, two sugars." She stepped into the kitchen and inspected his handiwork on the counter. "Hope your coffee making is better than your sandwich making—you really know how to butcher a PB&J."

"You should see my grilled cheese." Ryan took Poppy's critique in stride as he poured two mugs of steaming caffeine.

"Oh, I think I peeled one of those off my shoe last night."

Poppy picked up a knife and a slice of bread and jumped in to help finish the kids' lunches. Even though they hated her, she couldn't let them go to school with wonky PB&Js.

Ryan placed a mug right in front of her work zone. "Here you go."

"Thank you." Poppy meant it. She could smell the

dark roast and the anticipation of taking a sip brought some joy to the morning.

"Yeah…uh…" Ryan sat down in front of some paperwork, clearly looking for the right words. The collar of his light blue button down peeked from beneath a dark blue sweater. It had twisted slightly askew.

Poppy understood exactly how the collar felt this morning. It seemed everyone was a bit off today.

As Ryan stuttered, Poppy realized he might need the coffee even more than she did. And it had taken everything she had to get out of bed this morning and come back to face the Larson kids.

But she'd committed. Now, she was counting on the coffee to help her keep that commitment. "Rough night?" she asked.

"Uh, crowded night. Both kids ended up sleeping in my bed."

"Impromptu slumber party—love it!"

"More like 'Nightmare Patrol.' Spiders." Ryan flipped through the pages that filled the folder in front of him.

Suddenly, Poppy felt low. Coffee couldn't fix this guilt. Would she ever be able to do and say the *right* thing around here? "My fault."

Ryan casually dismissed her assessment of the situation. "No. Standard operating procedure." He closed the folder and slipped it in his briefcase. "So, you're living with Megan and the boys?"

"Temporarily." Poppy spread jelly on the last sandwich.

There was no mistaking the grin on Ryan's face. "Temporarily for Them?"

"My brother-in-law's in the military. When he shipped out, I moved in to help with the kids."

"That's really nice," Ryan said.

Poppy nodded in agreement. "It's nice for me too. A little break from living alone."

"So, you normally live alone?"

First Megan, now Ryan. Why was everyone so vicariously interested in her love life—or rather, her un-love life? "Normally."

"So, you're single…temporarily."

Did every guy she worked for have to start hitting on her? Weren't there any attached guys to work for in Seattle? Someone safe who wouldn't make her feel inadequate about her inability to commit to anyone or anything?

But she was working on that by sticking with this very job, she reminded herself.

"That would be correct." Poppy didn't mean to sound short, she just didn't know what else to say. She barely knew Ryan. And he *was* still her boss, even if it was for a short time. Her rules still applied.

"Sorry, I—I don't mean to pry. It's just you'd fit well into our test group."

"What?" Test group? Now that was one she hadn't heard before.

"My app. Food with Friends." Ryan pointed to

his smartphone. "So, say you're dining alone, and you log into our app. You can find other people nearby that are dining alone and don't want to. Boom. You're having food with friends."

Relief washed over Poppy. He wasn't hitting on her. He was just talking about his job again. For once, she was grateful that Ryan was a workaholic. "Sounds kind of amazing. Better than Food with Enemies."

"Oh, that's my next app." They both laughed at the same time. "Anyway, this company, Yamoharo Global, is considering buying us, which would expand us into foreign markets."

Poppy grabbed a marker and began to label the lunch bags. She could almost feel Ryan's enthusiasm for his product. "So, it's kind of huge?"

"Yeah, my big presentation for it is next Friday night."

"Halloween?"

"Yeah…" A frown crossed Ryan's face and he suddenly lost all traces of the confidence in his product that had been there only moments before. "I forgot about that. I don't think the Japanese celebrate it."

"Well, we do celebrate it here." Poppy felt that, for the kids' sake, she needed to remind Ryan. Without any decorations anywhere in the Larson home, it seemed like fall and Halloween didn't even make it on the calendar.

Ryan's phone beeped. He looked at the phone and swiped. His eyes scanned whatever had popped up on the slick screen. "I've gotta run."

"Here!" Poppy handed him a brown paper bag labeled "Ryan."

Ryan picked it up with his left hand. His right still carried his phone tightly. "What's this?"

Poppy couldn't keep a smile away. "PB&J made by a professional."

She couldn't tell if he was laughing at the fact that she expected him to brown-bag it like one of the kids or the jazz hands she used to emphasize her professional-grade lunch skills. Either way, it made her happy to see him appreciate the lunch.

"Ah, thank you."

She felt like she'd finally done something right. "You're welcome. Have a good one!"

"Good luck." The phone rang again, almost on cue, as Ryan walked out the door.

"Thanks," she called after him. Poppy realized she might have to deal with the kids, but at least she wasn't responsible for Ryan's phone. The constant ringing and beeping would drive her nuts.

With Ryan gone, Poppy was alone in the house with the kids. If she put a smile on her face, maybe they wouldn't see how fearful she was of another day like yesterday. Kids could smell fear. They latched on to it like sharks. Or something like that. She was pretty sure she'd read that on the Internet somewhere.

"Zoe! Zach! Almost time for school!"

No fear, Poppy. No fear. Fake it till you make it.

It didn't take long to get the kids loaded in her midnight black Saab. The morning came with the perfect fall air again, so Poppy decided to put the convertible top down for the drive to school.

Outside, birds chirped and other kids called to each other as they walked down the sidewalks. The neighborhood felt alive and full of bright cheerfulness.

Inside the car, however, the kids never said a word.

The silence made Poppy go into chatter mode. Maybe if she talked enough, one of the kids would hear something that would prompt them to let their guard down and speak. But as she turned into the driveway in front of the school, neither Zoe nor Zach had let out a single peep.

The school had clearly been here for decades. The building was low and squat, and a pavilion-style porch wrapped around the building. The sidewalks were shaded with awnings overhead. Mercer Elementary would have seemed like a trip into a time warp, but the brick had all been painted a warm taupe color, and hand-colored pictures had been taped in every window.

Instead of looking like the place her parents went to school, Mercer Elementary looked like the perfect place to feel secure while you learned. In fact, Poppy thought she wouldn't mind bringing her own brown bag out here and sitting under one of the old trees that shaded the lawn.

"Okay! Elementary school! I used to love it! My favorite subject was art class. And lunch! Who's your art teacher? Boy or girl? My art teacher's name was Miss A."

The minute Poppy's foot hit the brake, the kids began to unbuckle. They got out of the car without answering any of Poppy's overly enthusiastic questions. Poppy got out to walk them inside, but both kids passed by her with military-like precision, leaving her to stand next to the Saab as she became more aware of the sting of the redness climbing up her cheeks. "We'll talk later…um…we'll finish this later…"

Poppy slid back into the car, hoping no one noticed what just happened. Suddenly, she felt something squishy under her right leg.

"What is…" She reached a hand underneath her. "Oh, gross."

Poppy pulled out one of her professional-grade PB&J sandwiches. It had been pulled apart and left peanut-butter-side-up. Specifically, it was the one from the bag that had been labeled "Zoe."

Day two was not looking like it would shape up any better than day one. Poppy pulled out her cell phone and swiped until she found her sister's number.

But consolation was not to be. After two rings, the pre-recorded message began to play. "Hi, it's Megan. Please leave a message."

"Hi, you've gotta call me back." Poppy could hear the desperation in her own voice as she poured out her frustration to the voicemail. "I *literally* just sat in a peanut butter and jelly sandwich. These kids hate me. So, I don't know what I'm going to do."

She didn't want to admit to her sister that she wanted to cry into her gauzy black and white scarf—especially since Megan had no idea Poppy had pulled it out of her closet this morning without permission. But even with all the failures of the past few weeks—leaving the yoga class, practically dropping pizza dough on her face, running from the craziest date ever—nothing made her feel quite as hopeless as this moment.

She couldn't just run away from this. She couldn't just pivot and find herself elsewhere.

Poppy had committed to this job, as awful as it was. It was her place for the foreseeable future. But how could she stay in a role that made her want to cry? The minute that little pigtailed grouch, Zoe, saw she'd gotten to the latest nanny, that would be the point of no return. Poppy would have no chance with these kids.

Poppy turned her head as she sighed into the phone and focused her attention on the hundreds of hand-drawn pumpkins that decorated the windows at the front of the school. Halloween was just around the corner. All October 31 signaled to Ryan was the date of his much-anticipated presentation. But Poppy knew the kids didn't think of it that way. And they needed some fun in their lives. Maybe this year, the end of October could be filled with treats for the Larson kids. No more tricks. No more goblins.

No more of life's messes and changes that were out of their control.

"Never mind," Poppy said to Megan's voicemail. "I just got an idea."

Clinging to a shred of hope, Poppy hung up the

phone. Now to just wait until school dismissed. She turned the car left out of the school parking lot and headed back to Megan's house. Poppy wanted to grab her yoga mat. She needed to find a little peace while she passed the time until this afternoon.

At three o'clock, Poppy found herself back in the same traffic circle in front of the elementary school. But pick up, she vowed, as she looped into the concrete waiting zone, would wind up far different from drop off.

It had to. Something inside Poppy told her this was her last chance to connect with these kids. If any more time passed, attitudes would harden and solidify and she'd just be playing catch-up for the rest of the month.

Poppy couldn't live like that. She needed harmony in her life like she needed the crisp fall air, sunshine, and a good Washington-grown apple.

Zoe filed out the front doors first, twisting the fringe on her black-and-teal checked scarf. Her eyes opened wide as she saw Poppy casually leaning against the Saab.

"You're back," she said, with a mix of surprise and disdain.

Poppy put her plan in motion. No matter what Zoe said or did, Poppy would keep her joy. She would keep her sunshine. And eventually, that light had to wear down Zoe's defenses.

It just had to.

"Yep. How was school?"

"It was okay," Zoe said, giving a shrug for non-committal emphasis.

"I had a great day." Poppy said, with slightly exaggerated happiness. "I sat on the most delicious peanut butter and jelly sandwich."

She wanted Zoe to know that the prank hadn't brought her down.

Before Zoe had a chance to reply, Zach came running out. A smile was plastered across his face.

Good, thought Poppy. *Maybe I'll only have to kill one young Larson with kindness.*

"Miss Greene let us watch cartoons after lunch." Clearly, Zach's day had been made with just a little animation.

Memories came flowing back to Poppy from the happier parts of her own childhood. "I had a Miss Greene in second grade!"

Zach's eyes twinkled with excitement. "Maybe this is the same Miss Greene."

"What is she…about a hundred by now?"

"No, she's fifty," Zoe interjected, then cocked an eyebrow as she threw a verbal dagger. "Probably about your age."

"You think I'm fifty?" Of everything these kids had said or done to Poppy during the last twenty-four hours, she knew that one would stick with her the longest. Fifty? Almost double her actual age? This kid knew how to go for the jugular. It was like living in the elementary school version of *Mean Girls*. They learned early these days.

The corner of Zoe's mouth corkscrewed upwards with a slight snarl. "Probably sixty."

Poppy dusted off her hands. "Okay guys, little field trip before we go back home. Now, I can't lie—there are going to be spiders. But they're going to be fun spiders. I promise."

Surprisingly, Zach headed straight for the car. She had him at the word "fun."

Now it was time to work a little magic on Zoe. But wasn't that what Halloween was all about? Fun and a little magic?

Poppy was ready to stir up a spook-tacular afternoon and get these kids on her team once and for all.

"Halloween everything!" Poppy declared as they walked through the streamers that lined the front door to the local party supply store.

Zach's steps slowed to about half-pace as he took it all in. "Wow."

"Pretty cool, huh? Spooky." Poppy stopped and pulled out the largest shopping cart the store offered. She was ready to do some damage on these festooned aisles. "We're gonna need a cart—but I'm drivin'."

Glitter caught Zoe's eye as they turned down a row in the middle of the store.

Finally, the moment Poppy had been waiting for happened: Zoe uncrossed her arms.

Freed from the gesture of displeasure, she reached

out and picked up part of a costume and handed one to Poppy. "Hmm. These masks are really sparkly."

A rainbow of feathers in unnaturally bright colors fanned out across the top of the mask. The maroon velvet fabric was trimmed in gold sequins.

Immediately, Poppy played along. She held the mask up to her face and tried to catch Zach off-guard. "Aaaaaah…boo!"

Instead of being scared, he giggled. So far, so good.

"Oh, hey, this could look cool over the front door!" Poppy grabbed a string of plastic jack-o-lantern lights.

Zach found a complementary set of skull lights. "And these too!"

Poppy tossed them in the cart. If an item brought either of the kids joy, it would be coming back to the Larson house. That was the rule she'd set for today. "Yes! Pumpkins and skeleton heads go together like peanut butter and jelly."

"I'm going to find some headstones!" Zach ran to the end of the aisle, then turned the corner and headed for the lawn décor section.

"Our mom used to decorate for Halloween all the time…and then she got sick." Zoe's fingers trailed across the tops of paper pumpkin decorations.

Poppy wished she could see the little girl's face. "I'm sorry."

"It's okay. It was a long time ago. I don't really remember her. And Zach doesn't either."

The bravery came through loud and clear in Zoe's voice. She'd been through so much. Poppy wanted to hug Zoe but held back. A hug would be too much, too soon. She needed to keep the spiderweb-thin truce that had been declared once they walked in the Halloween store together.

"I bet you two had a lot of fun together."

Zoe quickly shifted subjects without replying. She saw a display that caught her eye. "Hey, look at these. My friend had these last year—her pumpkins looked amazing."

"We definitely need a pumpkin-carving kit. Actually, we need three. Too many pumpkins out there needing faces." Poppy loved carving pumpkins. And it seemed like the kids did, too. The idea of putting a face on a pumpkin had gotten the tiniest of chuckles out of Zoe. It felt like a small turning point.

This plan was working. Finally. Something was working.

Poppy never thought she'd find a little slice of her zen while being surrounded by skeletons and goblins. They didn't teach you that in yoga instructor school.

A moan came from the next aisle over. Zoe scampered around the corner, and Poppy quickly followed. Zach stood in the middle of the aisle, transfixed by an oversized, stuffed spider that had been wrapped around a pole and liberally topped off with some fake spider webbing.

"Oh, buddy—that's not real. It's not real." Poppy reached out and rubbed his shoulder reassuringly to let him know he wasn't alone. "It's okay."

"I know, but it's so scary." The fear in his voice

came through loud and clear. But at least this time, he hadn't run away.

Progress.

A rainbow clown wig on a shelf caught Poppy's eye. She grabbed it and threw it on the spider's fuzzy, black head.

"How 'bout now?" she asked Zach. "Hard to look spooky when you've got a wig on your head, huh? Although you've never met my aunt Eleanor..."

Both of the kids laughed.

"All right—what else do we need? Everything!" Poppy said with a small squeal. This was fun. She enjoyed seeing the smiles on the kids' faces. "Next stop, zombie aisle."

"I love zombies! Yay!" Zach gave a big cheer as he took off running.

Poppy pulled the basket up alongside Zoe. Something wasn't making sense. "Wait. Spiders, no. But zombies—he loves?"

"He's complicated."

Listening to Zach's excitement and seeing Zoe's smile made Poppy realize one thing for certain. These kids weren't complicated. They just needed a little undivided attention and unconditional love.

And she could be just the nanny to give that to them.

Temporarily, at least.

The Parcel Technologies offices bustled with activity.

Everyone could feel the spirit of hustle in the air. Even the developers who were letting off steam at the foosball table in the corner were turning the handles with far more force than usual.

Jean, the assistant who'd been with Ryan since the beginning, knocked on the door. When she didn't get an acknowledgement from her boss, she stuck her head in his office.

"Miss Morwell's on her way up."

Ryan looked up from his laptop, but never stopped typing. The emails never stopped coming in. He worried that there would never be a time when he felt caught up—much less a time when he could get ahead. "Thank you, Jean."

Within a minute, a tall brunette leaned against the doorframe. Her hair was pulled back in a sleek bun and her white designer suit was trimmed in inch-wide stripes of black leather. It had been cut to fit her like a glove. Everything about her radiated control and competence. Just by taking an offhand glance in her direction, it wasn't hard to figure out Abigail Morwell was at the top of her game.

"Do you ever stop working?" she asked.

*Touch*é. Ryan returned the volley. "Says the woman who sent me thirty emails on her flight back from Tokyo."

"Says the man who answered all of those emails in the middle of the night." Abigail had no problem giving as good as she got.

"Well, I'm efficient." Ryan decided to play it off.

He was a workaholic and he knew it. He just didn't have to publicly admit to it.

"It's one of your *many* attributes."

Wait. Was Abigail flirting with him? No one had flirted with him since Laurie leaned over and asked to borrow a pencil during a college calculus class. At least not that he noticed. Admittedly, he was out of practice.

Ryan wasn't even sure he'd know how to flirt back anymore. He'd packed away that part of his life a long time ago.

Abigail made herself comfortable in the chair across from Ryan's desk. "So…good news. Higashimoto loved the app. If we nail this presentation, they are *aaaallll* in. And you, my friend, are giving the presentation."

She leaned across the desk and made straight-on eye contact.

Ryan readjusted his position in his leather executive chair.

"Me? No—no." He wasn't sure if it was the idea of giving this make-it-or-break it presentation to Higashimoto and his team that made him squirm or the way Abigail delivered the verdict. "Look, you're the one who brokered the deal. It should be you."

"No. Ryan, you found an amazing way to connect people, and you need to be up front on this." Abigail reiterated her position on the matter.

"Yeah—I think you should be the one."

She blew off his objections and turned around the silver-framed photo on Ryan's desk.

"Aww, so cute. Zoe and Zach, right?" She tapped the glass over the image of him and the kids smiling at the top of Independence Pass in Colorado last summer.

"You have a good memory." Her attention to detail clearly extended beyond high-powered business deals. But maybe this was how a good salesperson networked. Remember the little things so you could score the big goals. Maybe he needed to take a lesson from Abigail so he could start brokering his own international deals in the future without needing to bring in outsiders and consultants.

She said, "It must be challenging, trying to raise them alone."

Ryan laughed, remembering the sight of Poppy scrubbing juice from the carpet and the stories about spiders and corn cobs…and some overly-social goats.

There was Higashimoto and Yamoharo Global… and then there was being a parent to the most stubborn and precocious eleven- and eight-year-olds that had ever been born on this planet.

"You have no idea."

No sooner had Poppy shifted into park than the kids hopped out of the car. Squeals announced their arrival to the whole neighborhood. They were pumped and they didn't care which neighbors noticed.

"This is going to be the best Halloween house on the block," Zoe declared as she raced toward the front door, hands full of the day's purchases.

Zach followed close behind her. His volume exceeded all normal levels for a young boy. "Or the world!"

Poppy pulled the rest of the bags of loot from the trunk of the car. "Or the universe!"

She yelled right along with the kids. It wasn't so much the idea of decorating that had her adrenaline rising to a fever pitch. Sure, she loved the ideas in her head, and everything that was about to take place in the Larson home and across the Larson yard.

But even more, she loved the idea that she'd finally gotten through to the hearts of the Larson kids.

As she walked inside, she dumped her day's spoils next to the items the kids had brought in. Close to a dozen orange bags with black writing were strewn across the living room and kitchen. Poppy was glad that Ryan had bought a house with what Realtors and home improvement reality shows liked to call an "open-concept living space."

This full-on, Halloween-based charm offensive would need lots of space to reach its full potential. And the starting point was going to be organization.

They would need to use the living room, the kitchen, *and* the dining room. This was serious business.

"And now, for the first phase of Operation: Decoration. Zoe, please take all this candy into the kitchen—without dipping into the stash, please." Poppy handed Zoe one of the bags, weighted down with a year's worth of sugary goodness. "All right guys, organization is key. We need to take everything out, then decide which decorations go where. Bats, rats, and cats to the left. Ghosts and ghouls to the right."

She held up a skeleton without even looking over her shoulder. Zach came immediately and spirited it away to the proper station.

Poppy mentally patted herself on the back. Finally, she was nannying like a boss. A decorating boss.

After about an hour of organizing and strategizing, Poppy and the kids moved a large number of the decorations outside, where they would be put up for the neighborhood to see.

"This should go here. Put some leaves around that one. It looks spookier." Zoe gave clear instructions to her little brother as they created a small graveyard display with gray plastic headstones.

Poppy relished the sound of happiness. She and the kids were on the same team. Now, to sustain the harmony—or whatever it was they'd found between the three of them.

"Okay, brain trust...your thoughts?" She stood on a ladder and reached a string of lights toward the trim around the edge of the front porch.

Zoe studied the scene for a moment, then offered her advice. "Drape those like icing on a cake."

There was always room for cake in Poppy's world. "A Halloween cake!"

"Yeah," Zoe approved.

Relief flooded through Poppy's entire body—all the way to the tips of her fingers as they hung the lights in place. Maybe Megan had actually been right. Maybe Poppy was good at this. Maybe, just maybe, she'd be able to keep her commitment to the Larsons without counting down the days...or hours and minutes and seconds, like yesterday.

After multiple strands of lights had been installed across the Craftsman-style front of the house and over the shrubs and landscaping, Poppy cruised over to where the kids were still focused on the grass-based decor. "Okay, bag of bones—coming in. This lawn needs more skeleton."

"That's how Mom used to do the lights." Zoe looked back at the house with a wistful smile. "She made the lights over there look like candy corn."

"I love candy corn." Poppy wanted to encourage the good memories of the kids' mother. Something inside told Poppy that honoring her would be good for the kids. "Sounds like your mom was really good at Halloween."

"She was." Zach's heart came out in his voice.

Zoe scoffed. "You were too young to remember, Zach."

"I saw a picture of her dressed like Chair at the Oscars." Zach didn't let his sister get the best of him. Instead, he defended the memory he treasured.

"Chair?" Poppy looked down at him, slightly puzzled. "Wait. Do you mean Cher? That is such a good idea for a costume." She laughed at the thought of Cher's infamous Bob Mackie black dress and headpiece.

If only Poppy could turn back time, too. She would have done so many things differently yesterday so she could've started off on the right foot with these kids. Mostly, she would have listened instead of insisting they go-go-go.

But she was listening now. And the kids were opening up to her. Together, they were making new memories.

Zoe turned to Poppy. "Are you dressing up for Halloween?"

"Of course I am!" Poppy laughed. As though there could ever be any doubt.

"As what?" Zoe stuck one more bony skeleton hand in the ground, then arranged the fingers.

Poppy waggled a plastic foot at Zoe in a gesture of mock scolding. "I'm not going to tell you! I can't promise it'll be as cool as Chair...but I'm gonna try."

Her stomach growled just a little. They'd been out here for more than two hours. Turning to a bag just behind them, Poppy reached in and pulled out a plastic baggie of frozen green grapes.

"Okay—snack time! Who here likes eyeballs?"

"Me." Zoe plucked out one and popped it in her mouth with a crunch.

Zach was less eager. "They aren't real eyeballs, are they?"

Poppy held the bag open for him. She wanted this shy boy to come out of his shell a little bit and try some new things. "Maybe they are. Why don't you taste one and tell me? Does it taste like an eyeball?"

With a slightly nervous squint, Zach pulled out a grape and then ate it.

"Yeah," he declared.

"So, you like eyeballs, huh? Are they your favorite food?" Poppy reinforced his small triumph.

Zach nodded with a smile and took several more grapes. "Yeah."

"Yeah, you like 'em. They're very nutritious." Suddenly, a skull swung into Poppy's field of vision, wielded by a grinning eleven-year-old. "What? Aaack!"

The sound of laughter filled the air. A bridge had been crossed. Poppy made a promise to herself never to go back.

And what was a promise, really, but a type of commitment?

This was a commitment she could keep. In her heart, she promised Zoe and Zach she would be there for them, there to help them build memories and find some of the joy that had been taken from them when cancer stole their mom away and long workdays kept their dad from home.

Poppy sat up a little straighter. She could commit. She *would* commit. These kids deserved no less.

Later that night, the house just felt cozier. Lights twinkled in the yard. Candles flickered inside jack-o'-lanterns. Something spook-tacular had indeed come to the Larson house, and so far, everyone seemed to benefit from the newly-created display to celebrate the upcoming holiday.

Zach crashed right after dinner. Poppy had to carry him up the stairs and tuck him in.

Zoe, on the other hand, seemed to be wired. A happy sort of electricity flowed through her. Sensing that she wouldn't be able to get Zoe to bed for a little while longer, Poppy let her stay up and help with dishes and cleaning up the whirlwind left behind from the day's decorating.

"Thanks for drying, even though I know it's a ploy to stay up later." Poppy swiped a sponge around the inside of a bowl.

Zoe wiped the front of a plate. "How do you know?"

"Because you have a dishwasher, smartypants." Poppy gave Zoe a playful hip-check.

"Hey! I just want to see my dad's face when he sees all the decorations." Zoe beamed.

Inside her heart, Poppy beamed too. She'd not only gotten through to both of the Larson children, but they'd all been able to really bond today. The simple joy of making the season special had fused them together like the three colors of candy corn.

"I know—me too." Poppy couldn't keep a smile off her own lips. "What face do you think he's going to make? I think he's going to be like 'uh…'"

Poppy crossed her eyes and twisted her features into the goofiest expressions she could.

Zoe waved off Poppy's attempt. "No, no… I think he's going to be like…"

She dropped her jaw and gave an impression of total shock, then slowly leaned back like she was going to fall over.

Just as they were getting into serious teasing territory, Zach appeared on the landing of the stairs. In his flannel pajama pants and blue T-shirt, he looked completely vulnerable.

"Hey!" Poppy wanted to reach out and cuddle him. She wanted to put her hand in his mop of dark blond hair and give it a little scratch to make it all okay.

The corners of his mouth turned down with sadness and fear. "I had a bad dream."

"Spiders?"

Zach nodded in silent reply.

Poppy placed the bowl she'd been washing down in the sink and went to Zach without hesitation. "All right, c'mon kiddo. Back up."

She led him back to his room with a reassuring hand on his shoulder. "Okay, hop in."

Poppy gestured at the bed, but Zach hesitated. He crawled in slowly and clutched a well-worn green-and-white stuffed T. Rex to his chest. Poppy sat on the edge of the bed beside him.

"Do you see how it's darker on that side of the room?" Zach pointed the dinosaur's nose in the direction of the far corner.

He was right. The light from the hall didn't reach that side. Poppy nodded. "I do."

"I dreamed that I fell asleep looking at the dark, and that spiders came crawling out to eat me." Poppy could barely see Zach's eyes as he lifted his gaze; they were hooded by heavy eyelids.

"Oh, that does sound scary. But that was just a dream. There are no spiders here." She reached to the bedside lamp and clicked it on. "See?"

As Poppy turned the lamp back off, Zach asked a tentative question. "Can I sleep with the light on?"

The lamp had a powerful bulb under the oatmeal-colored shade. Poppy knew if she left it on, the little boy would never get back to sleep, nor would he get the rest he needed.

She thought for a moment, then proposed a different option. "Why don't you sleep with the door open, so you can see the hall light?"

"But I can't see that light." He wasn't interested in the compromise.

"Why not?"

Zach laid down the dinosaur and patted his left shoulder. "Because I sleep on my left arm."

"I have an idea. Hop out." Poppy flopped the pillow to the foot of the bed and tugged the quilt up, then pointed as she gave directions. "Head…here. Toes…here."

Zach scrambled around and crawled back up on the bed as asked. Poppy drew the thick white blanket with red stars around the boy's body, folding first one side, then the other. "Now, I'll wrap you up like a burrito…there you go." She ran her hands along the outline of his shape in the bed, securing the sheets snugly around him.

Poppy pointed to the lamp glowing in the hall, just adjacent to his room's door. "Now you can see the light—all night."

"You'll leave the light on—*all* night?" Zach craned his neck so he could double-check the promise Poppy had made.

"All. Night." Poppy made sure to reassure him with one final pat. She stroked the bangs falling on his forehead and felt herself sigh. Such a sweet boy. She wanted to do whatever she could to make things better for him. Less than forty-eight hours into this nanny gig, and she already felt like the protector she knew these precious kids needed. "Sleep well."

Another late night. And there would be many more to come. It made Ryan even more tired, just thinking about it.

He trudged up the driveway, eyes glued to his phone as he tried to read one more email before being forced to take a break when he walked in the house. Hopefully, Poppy would already have the kids in bed—it was a school night, after all—and he could get back to making edits on the presentation as soon as she left for the night.

He opened the door and pushed it shut with his free hand, not bothering to even turn around and lock it, since Poppy would just be headed back out shortly.

The lights in the kitchen were all on, and Poppy was wiping down the countertop. She smiled as he walked by.

"Hey…" he started.

Poppy looked up from her tidying and lifted her gaze to the nearby staircase.

Ryan paused and turned toward the stairs. Zoe was wearing her pajamas, but instead of being in bed, sat cross-legged on the landing. "Hey…what are you still doing up?"

He sat his phone and briefcase on the newly-shined counter.

Poppy took the blame for Zoe's late bedtime. "Oh, that's on me. I needed her help—cleaning."

"Oh." Ryan didn't believe a word of it. Zoe never cleaned unless there was something in it for her.

"Didn't you see the stuff outside?" His daughter smiled hesitantly, waiting for his reply.

What stuff? The grass and trees had been there since they moved in almost a decade ago. "Oh, I… uh—yeah."

Zoe's face lit up. Ryan knew he'd missed something big. He hadn't seen Zoe this excited about anything in ages. "So, what was your favorite?" she asked. "The goblins? The jack-o'-lanterns? Or the cats? Were you scared?"

Her litany came off with the same rapid-fire buzz as a swarm of mosquitoes.

"Uh…" How could he give an answer that would

meet Zoe's expectations? Ryan hadn't seen a darned thing in the yard.

Well, nothing except the blue glow of the screen of his smart phone and yet another email from Abigail Morwell.

He turned around to look at Poppy, who thankfully jumped to his rescue.

"You scared your dad speechless!"

Ryan wanted to high-five her. That was a good save. Poppy was quick on her feet. He liked that about her. He turned back to Zoe with a half-laugh and an open-hands gesture, trying to indicate that Poppy's assertion was correct.

Zoe saw right through it. He should have known.

His daughter's voice increased in volume with every word. "He didn't even notice. He never notices anything!"

She ran up the stairs with a speed only equaled by Olympic medalists.

"Zo—" Ryan started to call after her—then he heard the door slam. The loud thunk spoke an encyclopedia's worth of volumes.

"I guess I'd better go up and talk to her," Ryan said. He didn't know what else to do, but he knew he needed to think of something, quickly.

How could he have all the answers for Yamoharo Global and Higashimoto, yet have nothing for his own kids?

On autopilot, he started to gather up his phone to take with him, but Poppy reached out and clapped a hand over the ever-present device on the counter. "I'll hold on to your phone."

"Thanks."

About ten minutes later, Ryan came back downstairs. He'd given a sincere apology to Zoe and tucked her in bed, but he still didn't know if he'd truly made amends.

He'd disappointed her. Deep in his heart, little flakes of ice began to stick.

Poppy was waiting in the kitchen with a mug of fresh coffee in each hand. "So, how'd it go?"

"She's pretty mad at me." *Good one, Captain Obvious.*

"Just wait until she's a teenager."

The small flakes became icicles. Poppy had just voiced his greatest fear. He had no idea how to raise a pre-teen girl, much less a full-fledged teenager. There was no manual for this. He'd always been prepared for Laurie to handle these things. "Don't say that! That's mean."

"Coffee." Poppy pointed at the mug like she was a sergeant issuing an order. "Unless you need something stronger."

The one thing he needed was to give Poppy the credit she deserved as well. "Thanks for decorating with them. It sounds like you guys had a lot of fun."

Poppy came around and sat on the stool next to him, pulling her own steaming cup close. "We did."

Ryan took a sip. He picked up his phone and

twirled it absently without looking at it. It was his own adult fidget spinner.

"Not that it's any of my business, but..." Poppy pointed straight at the spinning rectangle. "Is that phone glued to your hand? Do you need to see a doctor?"

"Yeah." She had him dead to rights, and Ryan knew it. But what else could he do? The smartphone was his mobile office. He could talk to people around the world, read emails, handle problems instantly before they became emergencies. "I just have to make it through this presentation. If I can get through that—if it goes well—it'll free me up so I can spend more time with the kids. You know, quality time."

Poppy probably didn't believe it, but Ryan knew he spoke the truth. His kids mattered to him. They were his *why*. They were the reason he was pursuing this global opportunity. It was his chance to make sure they were taken care of for the future.

It was his chance to make good on his last promise to their mother.

Zoe and Zach were never far from his mind, or his heart—even though he was often far from them physically.

"I understand." Poppy nodded.

Maybe she did understand—at least as much as she could, seeing as how she hadn't known him or the kids for very long.

"Although I'm not sure they do," she continued.

"You know, they've been talking about their mom and Halloween."

Ryan almost dropped his phone. The kids hadn't mentioned Laurie to him in ages.

Poppy gestured at the paper decorations that had been hung over the fireplace, then over to the skeleton that took up the full length of the pantry door. "Maybe celebrating the holiday could be a way for them to remember how funny she was."

The assessment caught Ryan off-guard. "How do you know she was funny?"

"Because she dressed up like 'Chair' from the Oscars." Poppy grinned.

"Yeah, she did. The kids told you that?"

Poppy's smile continued to glow. "Zach did. He seems to remember more about her than you'd think, considering his age. He wants to remember her. Zoe does too. She told me several times that we needed to do the decorations a certain way because that's how her mom styled them. You must really miss her."

Ryan looked down at his phone. He didn't want to admit the truth. Not to himself, and not to the astute woman across from him. But as much as he missed Laurie, he couldn't bring her back. The only thing he could do was to continue moving forward—both for him and for the kids. "Nothing's easy, right?"

"You know, my sister said there's a Halloweek party at the kids' school," she offered.

"Halloweek?" Ryan wondered if the nanny had misspoken.

"Halloween week. Halloweek." Poppy made a funny face and rolled her eyes. "It's a thing."

"Okay." He wondered where she was going with this.

Ryan couldn't help but notice that a light had begun to twinkle in Poppy's eyes. He recognized that spark—he'd had it himself the moment he'd gotten the idea for Food with Friends. The smile that came over Poppy's face lifted the corners of her mouth, her cheeks, and even the edges of her eyelashes.

Her face came alive with a radiant glow.

It took Ryan aback to realize how much she already cared about his kids. The sentiment was written plainly across every inch of her face.

"Anyway, they have to bring homemade cookies. So maybe, tomorrow night, after work, you could help us bake them."

He gave Poppy a ten for her idea to bring them all together. Unfortunately, he had to score himself a zero for execution.

"Ugh, I won't be home until late. I have this dinner with a colleague." He paused. Abigail had set everything up and given him a time and a place. But she hadn't come out and specified the purpose of the out-of-office dinner meeting. "I guess you could call her that."

"Her, huh?" Poppy was astute. Not much got past her.

"Yeah. To be honest, I'm not sure if it's Food with Friends or an actual *date*."

Poppy stood up from the chair she'd been sitting in and began to loop her thin scarf around her neck. "Hmm…who suggested the dinner?"

"She did."

"And what kind of food?" Poppy slid her arms in her leather jacket.

Ryan shrugged. "Italian."

"Italian's probably a date."

She'd just confirmed what he'd been avoiding admitting to himself. "Yeah?"

"Yeah. I've had my share of Italian restaurant dates. Most of them start with antipasto and end with me anti-everything." Poppy wrinkled her nose. She gave a laugh, but Ryan could tell she found nothing funny about the memories.

Poppy swung her purse over her shoulder. "But all of this is research for this app I've been working on."

"Which would be?" Now she was speaking his language.

"Bad Dates and Broccolini."

"I think I can get you financing for that."

"Great." She gave another strained laugh. "All right."

Poppy clapped her hands and turned around for the door, effectively ending all conversation about first dates.

"Thanks again." He followed her to the door and locked it behind her.

Ryan wondered why Poppy's demeanor changed so suddenly when he'd mentioned the evening with

Abigail. Had she been that disappointed that he wouldn't be there to make cookies with the kids?

Or had there been something else she wasn't saying?

What surprised him even more, though, was when he wondered what it would be like to take Poppy to a cozy restaurant illuminated with the dim light of a candle in the middle of the table and to listen to her razor-sharp wit over their own shared plate of antipasto.

Would she still be anti-everything afterwards? Or would she find herself in support of a second date with a widower and two precocious kids who loved Halloween decorations?

Phone back in his hand, Ryan decided to call it a night. He turned out the downstairs lights and tried to ignore the sound of an eavesdropper's footsteps running back up the stairs.

What he couldn't ignore was the way the idea of a date with Poppy wouldn't leave his mind.

Chapter Four

THE NEXT DAY, AFTER SCHOOL, Poppy and Zoe mixed and measured in the kitchen, making cookie dough for the Halloweek party treats.

Zoe had fallen back into her quiet routine, but this time, Poppy could sense that the reticence was not due to the presence of a nanny.

"Do you think my dad's in love with that Abigail person?" Zoe's question came out haltingly.

Poppy tipped a rounded spoonful of brown sugar into her mixing bowl. "Abigail?"

"I saw her name in his phone." Zoe stopped mixing her dough and looked up at Poppy. Her eyes took on an almost puppy-like quality. "Leslie Mintz said that when her parents got divorced, her dad went out to dinner with a woman, and then six months later, they were married."

Grabbing the next two ingredients, Poppy decided to stall. Last night, Ryan wasn't even sure the dinner qualified as a date—despite all the signs pointing to yes, as Poppy had pointed out. But if even he seemed unsure, Poppy didn't see much hope for her ability to set Zoe's mind at ease with any level of certainty. *Who knows…* was probably not the answer Zoe's mind—or heart—sought.

"Cream. Sugar. Mish the two together." Poppy tried to buy some time to think.

"All right." She reached for a measuring cup, but Poppy stopped her.

"Nope. No measuring cups. I don't believe in measuring." Maybe turning the focus back to baking would distract Zoe and get her off this train of thought.

"How do people know when they're in love?"

Nope, apparently not.

"You're asking me? I'm single." Poppy tried to act like she was laughing it off, but inside, she felt like a flower withering without enough water. Zoe needed the advice of a female role model—a mother figure—here, and in this area, Poppy had none to give.

Well, maybe one piece of advice. *Figure out how to deal with commitment, kid.*

Zoe wouldn't be deterred. She kept the questions coming. "Yeah, but you're like forty, right?"

"Ha." That punch went right below the belt. "Last week you said I was fifty."

"You look younger the more I get to know you." The little girl in the teal-and-white chevron patterned apron smiled broadly. It was a genuine smile, a friend's smile. Poppy took that little victory to heart and treasured it.

Most of Poppy's life had been headed in the wrong

direction lately. She decided to appreciate the fact that at least Zoe's assessment of her seemed to be on the right path. "Let me know when I get to my twenties. We'll have a party."

"Yeah." Zoe giggled for a moment as she stirred the contents of her bowl, then stopped abruptly and turned her face upward. "Do you think my dad's going to fall in love with Abigail?"

"Oh, I wouldn't worry about that." Poppy didn't want Zoe to stress about things she couldn't control. But how could she tell this little girl who'd already been through so much to blow off what Poppy knew had to feel like a very real fear?

"I'm not worried. I just…" Zoe hesitated and furrowed her brow over her dark eyes. "I don't get how people know."

"Hmm…" Poppy didn't have a lot of love experience. But she did have life experience. And she'd seen the amazing marriage her own sister enjoyed. Maybe she could pull together an acceptable answer. "I think you know you're in love when you see something really beautiful and your first thought is 'I want them to see it too.' Or when they make you laugh. Or when you love what they love because they love it."

As she finished her assessment, Poppy felt that flower in her soul curl up even more. She'd dismissed every single guy she'd ever gone out with. Usually she had a reason to avoid the second date already justified in her mind before the appetizer course had finished.

Was she her own worst enemy?

In her mind's eye, Poppy saw the reflection of her life as clearly as if Zoe was holding a mirror instead of sugar cookie dough.

The reason she struggled to commit was because she sabotaged herself.

But why? Why would Poppy, who loved joy and happiness and the simple things in life, go out of her way to steal her own joy and ensure that her happiness was only fleeting and never a happily-ever-after kind of thing?

Poppy had been able to give Zoe a passable answer for her questions.

Unfortunately, she knew she didn't have an equation that made sense for herself.

"Have you ever been in love?"

"Like that? Not really. Not yet."

And probably never.

Man, she had to get them both focused back on baking. "Okay, crack some eggs. Pick one."

Zoe pointed to a brown egg in the middle of the carton. "I choose you."

"Not that one." Poppy yanked the carton away with a laugh. "Just yolk-ing."

Just joking. Poppy wished her heart had been just joking. Sarcasm was her love language. It would have been fine if her heart had been just poking the bear, just trying to get a reaction.

But she knew that wasn't the case. The still, small voice inside spoke truth.

Poppy wanted to just laugh and make dumb food

jokes with Zoe, but she couldn't shake the nagging fear inside. Had she gotten on board the commitment train too late? Would she be going through this life change, proving she could be a dependable person, in it for the long-term, only to discover it was too late for it to really matter? Had she missed her chance before she ever realized just what she needed to do?

The lights were low in the trattoria located in a historic storefront in a trendy part of town. Once again, it seemed that Poppy had been right. This wasn't a meet-up-after-work-to-discuss-the-day's-conference-calls kind of place. This was an atmosphere-and-Pinot-Grigio-by-the-bottle-followed-by-a-shared-Tiramisu kind of place.

How had he not seen this coming?

Quite honestly, he hadn't seen a lot of things coming lately. Heck, he hadn't even seen Halloween coming. He'd accepted the date of the Yamoharo Global presentation without even thinking about how that would affect his kids.

Thank goodness for Poppy. Not only had her strange date rating scale tipped him off to Abigail's real intention for this evening, but her love of Halloween had swooped in and changed the entire atmosphere of the house.

She'd only been in his and the kids' lives for a few short days. And she was only theirs to keep temporarily. But with her knack for seeing things

Ryan was completely oblivious to, what would they all do when she was theirs no more?

Thank goodness for Poppy, indeed.

At least *temporarily*, life for him and the kids would make a little more sense.

Abigail laid her menu to the left side of the table, then leaned forward as she began to speak.

"Well, they offered me an executive position with a full benefit package. Health plan, housing, expense account…all the perks. But I said no. I mean, it's a great promotion. But I just can't see myself living in Tokyo."

Abigail raised her wine glass and took a long sip. Ryan looked straight at her, trying to move his focus back to the conversation in front of him instead of his thoughts about Poppy back at the house. Abigail had done so much for Parcel Technologies lately. He owed her at least his full attention.

"Well, it sounds like a tempting offer."

"I'm kind of hoping I'll get a better offer here." Her dark burgundy nail polish almost blended in with the color of the Cabernet Sauvignon in her wine glass.

Ding. With one sentence, Abigail confirmed what Poppy had known immediately.

Ryan felt like an idiot. Even after Poppy laid it all out, he still hadn't been one hundred percent sure that tonight was set up to be a date. *Larson, get in the game. She's wearing a slinky burgundy v-neck dress and she's wearing her hair down. Oh, and she's got on three times as much makeup as she usually wears. All the signs are there. Your powers of observation are about as functional as the blue screen of death on a computer.*

He couldn't wait to get this presentation over with so he could get back to his real life and not be completely consumed and distracted. In fact, the best way to do that was to take the opportunity now to nail down a few details that were on his mind. "Listen, about the presentation...I feel like you should probably—"

"How about we *don't* talk about business tonight?" Abigail's emphasis was unmistakable.

So was the way she leaned forward across the table, letting the deep neckline of the dress show off a hint of cleavage. None of the high-powered suits she wore in the office ever teased anything.

"Okay. Actually, I wasn't really sure whether this was a work thing—"

She cut him off. "If it was a work thing, would I be flirting so shamelessly?"

"So, you were flirting?"

"Wasn't it obvious?" She smiled broadly, inviting him to flirt back. At least he picked up on that.

Ryan wished he could offer her anything more than a nervous laugh in return. It had been a long time since he'd been on a date, but he remembered his younger years well. Flirting was supposed to be easy. Trying too hard was a death knell.

He didn't know if it was Laurie's memory, or something else entirely. But when it came to the modus operandi for this dinner, Ryan realized that not only was he not trying too hard, he wasn't trying at all.

And more specifically, he didn't feel like he really wanted to try.

But as to exactly why…well, he didn't know for sure. Wouldn't the kids benefit more from a family with a father and a mother, instead of a string of frazzled nannies? He hadn't thought much about dating since Laurie died. But here he was, on a date, with a woman who was clearly interested in him.

Maybe it was time to think about the future. Maybe it was time to try?

The waitress placed an oversized white platter of antipasto between Ryan and Abigail. Salami, fresh mozzarella, cured red peppers, artichoke hearts, Kalamata olives. Abigail said something and plucked an olive from the tray. Ryan didn't hear any of it. He just heard Poppy's summation of her first date experiences.

An hour or so later, Ryan pulled in the driveway. It felt good to be home. The decorations made the place look more inviting than it had in so many years. He'd forgotten what it looked like when a house had been transformed by love and laughter into so much more.

In one afternoon, Poppy had made their house a home again.

All the small talk he'd just engaged in with Abigail seemed so pointless. There was no place Ryan wanted to be more than right here, inside this home with his kids.

But he couldn't indulge the home-sweet-home fantasy. At least not for a little while longer. He needed to finish the Yamoharo deal. Then he could plan for how best to get on the dating train, now that it seemed to have pulled into the station without him realizing it. Hopefully, next month wouldn't be too late to buy a ticket.

Ryan came in the house and heard chatter back in the kitchen. Poppy and the kids sat around the kitchen table, surrounded by cookies and icing. Poppy balanced a gumdrop on her fingertip. Zoe plucked it from her and set it in a swirl of colorful icing atop a sugar cookie.

"Oh, you guys are still up?"

"Dad—come see." Zoe gestured at the three plates' full of cookies in front of them. "These are the best Halloween cookies ever."

"We got a little bit carried away," Poppy said, with far too much enthusiasm for it to be a real apology. "But—these are not just Halloween cookies. These are *educational* cookies."

Poppy had been dead serious with her choice of words, but Ryan still felt like he didn't make the connection. "I see skeletons, bats, haunted houses… how is that educational?"

"This skeleton cookie?" Poppy held out a cookie shaped roughly like a gingerbread man, but instead decorated with little white icing bones. "A celebration of science. There are two-hundred-and-six bones in the human body."

He couldn't argue with her there. Anatomy was useful to know. Plus, it was fun to play along with the ultra-earnest expressions she and the kids were wearing, clearly barely holding back laughter. "What about the bats?"

"Recently added to the endangered species list. A reminder of how important it is for us to care about our environment." The black-frosted bat had been trimmed with thin ribbons of green icing. They'd even drawn a goofy grin on the bat's face, complete with little sugary fangs.

Biology—or zoology or something. He could buy that. "And the haunted houses?"

"Okay, these are kind of Halloween-ish. But I prefer to think of them as houses with a past."

"Mmm—yeah, I don't know about that one." Ryan couldn't help but chuckle along with Poppy. *Well, she tried.*

A smile that glowed brighter than a jack-o'-lantern lit up his daughter's face. "Dad, will you come to the Halloweek party tomorrow? Pleeeease? It's at lunch. You hardly have to miss work."

His daughter had even applied logic, shooting down his most obvious objection before he had a chance to voice it. Ryan had to give Zoe credit. She might have a future in debate or public speaking.

In fact, maybe he could get her to make the presentation to Yamoharo Global. He didn't know Higashimoto well, but how could anyone say no to Zoe's grin and dimples and signature pigtail braids?

"I will try my very best." Zach gave the air a fist bump. The smiles on both his kids' faces pulled at his heartstrings.

Too bad his schedule was packed tomorrow. Even for lunch. But it was better that he keep that knowledge to himself. He couldn't bear to wipe the smiles from the kids' faces. He'd rather leave them with hope.

Ryan knew he couldn't be there at the party, but he was here right now. May as well make the most of it. He checked his watch to make sure the idea that just popped in his head would work. "Okay, now, if you guys hurry and get your pajamas on, we'll have enough time for two bedtime stories. But that means you have to go now."

"Yeah! Yeah!" Zach's enthusiasm leaped up another gear.

Poppy clapped and encouraged both of the kids like they were in the home stretch at a NASCAR race. "Go—go—go!"

Zoe took off for the stairs, leaving a trail of cookie crumbs in her wake. "C'mon, Zach. I'm going to beat you upstairs!"

Poppy began to straighten up the chaos left behind at the table. She pulled out a length of cling film and deliberately raised her gaze to Ryan's. "So, when you say, 'I will try my best,' does that really mean no?"

"Well, I've got a busy day tomorrow—" It sounded so pathetic coming out of his mouth, but it *was* the truth. Nothing he could do about that.

Poppy stood and came around the table. She got

close to Ryan and put her hand on her hip as she spoke. Ryan froze and put his full attention on her.

"Okay, listen. When I was little, my parents split up, and my mom was—is—is this total free spirit. Like, she always has some new hobby she's passionate about. But she never came to my soccer games—or my sister's choir recitals. Then there was my dad. He was really hard to communicate with. He's this super stoic man. But he always showed up. Who do you think I'm closer to?"

Ryan couldn't take his eyes off Poppy. She wore a powder-blue button-down shirt tucked into a pair of black cotton pencil trousers. She finished off the outfit with a pair of neat leather flats and a tiny silver necklace that winked as it caught the light from the lamp in the corner of the room. In his nine-to-five world, she'd be just another woman in a business casual outfit.

But something seemed irresistibly compelling about the deep passion in her voice as she scolded Ryan with a reminder of the two different paths of parenthood he could take. It felt different from any colleague he'd ever worked with or managed. He could almost imagine her as his partner in raising these kids, gently reminding him that he was about to make a costly mistake.

Poppy wasn't about profit and loss. She was about people and love.

And no bottom line mattered more than that. He knew it. He just wasn't doing a good job at showing it these days. Eventually, the kids would benefit from Parcel Technologies' success. They'd reap the rewards of Food with Friends.

But that was in the future. They needed investment of his time today.

"I will be there." He nodded solemnly, trying to work out the shifts of tomorrow's schedule around in his head. Ryan couldn't quite straighten it out right now, but he'd talk to Jean in the morning and get her to move some meetings around.

"Good." Poppy's smile was genuine. She cared.

"I'm really glad you're here." He meant it. Yesterday, Poppy had gotten him to put down his phone—no mean feat. And tonight, she'd gotten him to look more closely at things.

Including Poppy herself.

He leaned forward and raised a hand to one of her auburn curls. "You've got a little—sorry—" Ryan pinched at a bit of white tangled in the strands above her left ear. "You've got a little flour in your hair."

She smelled like sugar cookies. He wanted to keep hovering just inches away from her and take it all in, but Poppy pulled back ever-so-slightly.

"So—" Poppy began.

Ryan tried to transition the conversation at the same time. "So—"

The moment had crumbled like the edges of one of the cookies on the table.

"Was it a date?" Poppy turned her back to Ryan and picked up the roll of cling film again, tugging out a sheet large enough to wrap over the last plate of cookies.

Ryan answered honestly. "Turns out, it was."

The fact that he thought about Poppy all night as Abigail talked over wine and pasta…that fact, he kept to himself. He knew Poppy would think he was crazy. Out with one woman, thinking about another. That didn't seem right at all.

And yet, that's exactly how the evening played out.

"So, there might be date number two?" Poppy deftly wrapped the remaining cookies.

Ryan noticed the square set of her shoulders. He wondered why her usually bubbly personality had gone flat.

Her parents' divorce.

Using it as an example had to have dredged up painful memories. Poor Poppy—she'd clearly been carrying that around for a long time. Ryan hoped that one day, his kids wouldn't look back on their own childhoods and become chilled at the memories.

"Maybe."

Or maybe not. It depended on whether or not Ryan could stop thinking about flour and curls and the smell of sugar cookies.

"Cool." Poppy turned around with a smile that seemed larger than usual. "Well, I will see you tomorrow for the Halloweek party."

She didn't have to remind him. He knew what he needed to do. "Great. Thanks again."

"Yeah." Poppy sped past Ryan.

Was she afraid that if she slowed down, he'd reach out and touch her hair again? Man, he'd really messed up. Ryan grabbed his phone and checked tomorrow's calendar, trying to ensure that he'd at least get one thing right.

Chapter Five

ERCER ELEMENTARY SCHOOL KNEW HOW to throw a party, Poppy thought as she looked around the fully-decorated gym. No wonder they called this event "Halloweek." You couldn't fit this much fun and frou-frou into just one day.

Mylar ghost-shaped balloons floated everywhere, tied to the ends of tables and chairs. Two colorful tents with red-and-white striped roofs had been erected along the back wall. Strands of lights criss-crossed the open space.

A group of fifth-graders were whacking at a giant pumpkin piñata, and in the back corner, kids were cocooning parents and teachers with unending rolls of toilet paper as part of the "Mummy Wrap" game.

Poppy had been assigned management of a booth for baked goods. She felt just like a real Mercer parent—not just a token nanny—as she watched the kids play and shriek and generally have a good time.

Well, all of them except Zoe. Her young charge practically vibrated with nerves. She stuck close to

Poppy instead of venturing out across the bedecked gymnasium with her friends.

"You reminded Dad about the party, right?" Zoe's eyes were glued to the door which led to the parking lot.

Poppy tried to reassure her for the twenty-seventh time, but knew every word she uttered was falling on deaf ears. "Yes. Yes, he's coming."

Zoe looked down, a frown on her face. She rearranged a line of cling film-wrapped brownies. "Even though he has no time for Halloween?"

Poppy couldn't argue that fact. She'd seen first-hand how distracted Ryan was when he was with the kids and away from his office. Last night, he'd made them a promise, but Poppy worried that there were just too many promises he couldn't keep right now, despite any good intentions.

That said, she didn't want to make Zoe's anxiety climb any higher. "He's just forgotten how much fun it is. But we're going to remind him, right? Come on, help me pass out these cookies before I eat them all myself."

A group of kindergarteners came by and swarmed the booth for a sugary dose of sustenance.

"Here you go," Poppy said as she passed out chocolate chip cookies. Despite the noise and the crush of children and parents and teachers—and the occasional ghoul or goblin—Zoe continued to stare at the faraway set of metal doors, oblivious to anything else around her.

Ryan wanted to be the Little Engine Who Could today, but he was sliding back down the hill miserably.

Paul, his lead developer, had caught a bug in the programming this morning that kept Food with Friends from loading the same on a mobile device as it did on a computer. They'd hopped on a conference call with the technical team in India first thing this morning—and Ryan was still on the call. This was not the time to have the interface go wonky.

He spun in his desk chair and tapped the screen of the tablet on his desk.

Nope, it still loaded at the wrong aspect ratio. This had to get solved. Now.

But Ryan knew he needed to get off this call. Jean had managed to move this afternoon's meeting with marketing up to eleven-thirty so he could be out the door and headed for school by noon. If traffic cooperated, Ryan could be at Mercer Elementary by twelve-fifteen.

He'd blocked thirty minutes of time in his calendar to actually spend at the Halloweek party, then back to the car, back to the office, and back into a conference room. The HR team expected him at one. And then he'd be back on with Paul and the India tech team at two-thirty. The time difference meant the international team would be up all night trying to solve this problem, so Ryan had to stick to the new schedule.

"Listen, it's got to work flawlessly on all platforms.

Not just your phone. It's got to work on your laptop. It's got to work on your tablet—any device available to you."

They didn't see hurricanes up here in the Pacific Northwest, but Ryan could swear he was living in one right now.

Jean stuck her head in the door for the fourth time in the last fifteen minutes. This time, she ignored Ryan's hand waving her off.

"Ryan? They're waiting for you in the conference room."

He covered the microphone end of his phone's handset with his palm. "It's not eleven-thirty."

"No, it's eleven-forty-five. I've been reminding you since eleven."

He jumped up and headed for the door, still continuing the conversation. The black base of the landline phone skidded across his desk and wobbled as it began to tip off the edge. Ryan came to a halt, remembering he wasn't on his mobile.

"Hey—no—listen, I've got to call you back."

He hung up the receiver, grabbed his cell phone and a tablet, and rushed down the hall, mentally running down a list of every swear word he knew.

There was no way he would make the Halloweek party now.

"Where is he?" Poppy walked through the crowd, passing out cookies from a tray.

Megan plucked a cookie studded with M&Ms off the top of the stack. "He's probably stuck in traffic."

"No, he said he would be here." Poppy reiterated the promise Ryan made last night.

Megan took a step back. "You're getting—um—pretty involved here, aren't you?"

Poppy refused to make eye contact with anyone more than four feet tall—namely, her sister. "No—I—I'm thinking about the kids."

"I'm not just talking about the kids." Megan followed Poppy around doggedly, refusing to give up this bone of juicy conversation.

Poppy felt as though she'd been transported in time. Suddenly, she was back in elementary school again, annoyed with her older sister for teasing her about something stupid. And this was stupid. Ryan was her boss. How many times did Poppy have to explain her dating rules to Megan? "Don't do this again."

"Do you want to be an old maid?"

Poppy stopped and turned around. She couldn't *not* stare Megan down on that one. "Old maid? Really? Like, who says old maid?" She narrowed her eyes and tried to glare, but she wasn't sure if it worked.

Apparently, it didn't. Megan was not deterred. Not one single bit. "Oh, you're right. Is spinster better?"

"Spinster's better. I prefer spinster." Poppy plastered a fake smile on her face as she began handing out cookies left and right. Just like a good spinster with no chance for kids of her own would do.

"Look, I've known Ryan since the boys were in kindergarten. He's a great guy."

Why did Megan have to keep doing this? No matter how true her sister's observations were, Poppy refused to give her the satisfaction of agreeing to them.

Because that would mean she'd also have to admit the truth to herself.

"Yeah, he is. He's just not…" Poppy began placing cookies in a neat row in front of a group of kids playing a game called "Bean Bag Boo Bingo."

Megan swooped in and finished Poppy's sentence with a floppy, dismissive wave of her perfectly-manicured hand. "Not for you…"

"Dating someone else."

Got her. Surely Megan would stop now.

"Who?"

"Her name is Abigail." The mere acknowledgement of the other woman tasted like black licorice on Poppy's tongue as she spoke. Poppy hated black licorice. "They're colleagues."

"Oh. Well, that doesn't sound like much of a threat."

If the shoe had been on the other foot, Poppy knew she would have said the exact same line to her sister. But Poppy knew something Megan didn't. "They ate Italian food together."

"Well…" Megan took in a breath and paused. Now, she got it. "Maybe a little bit more of a threat."

"She's pretty. Actually, she's gorgeous." Poppy didn't want to admit the truth. Especially when she knew no one had ever said the same about her. All her life, she'd been "cute little Poppy."

Cute.

What woman wanted to be cute?

Cute never turned a man's head. Cute never got you commitment.

"Oh. You met her?"

"Nah—I Googled her."

Megan crossed her arms and leveled her gaze straight on Poppy.

Is it getting hot in here? Suddenly, it didn't feel anything like Seattle in the fall. "It means nothing. I Google a lot of people."

"Okay, well…I guess I can tell you." Megan gave a little laugh, then dismissed the entire discussion about Ryan and the gorgeous Abigail. She'd moved on. "I have another blind date for you."

Poppy had wanted to change the subject quite badly, but this wasn't what she'd had in mind as the next topic of conversation. "Does he already have his wedding tuxedo picked out?"

"Stop it." Megan was not amused.

Poppy couldn't resist one more jab at her sister's matchmaking track record. "Does he live with his mother?"

"You know, I'm going to get back to you on that one."

How about no?

It wasn't just time for a change of topic, it was time for a change of scenery. Poppy was ready to move on to something else entirely. Just then, her favorite second-grader walked by.

"Hey, Zach—I think I saw your name on the mummy wrap."

"Really?"

"Yeah. Zoe's over there." Poppy pointed back to the corner of the gym. Streamers of toilet papers waved as the vent overhead blew air across them. "You wanna go check it out?"

"Yeah." He gave a little squeal of excitement.

Poppy could tell her sister's feelings had gotten hurt. She shouldn't have teased. Megan only wanted what was best for Poppy. It wasn't her fault every single guy she knew in Seattle seemed to either be a total dweeb or a mama's boy.

Well, every single guy except Ryan Larson.

But he wasn't single anymore.

And she wasn't thinking about him like that. Poppy was only thinking of his kids, who needed some cheering up after their absentee father no-showed once again.

"You know who else is gorgeous?" Megan asked. "You are."

Poppy handed the last few cookies to her and gave her a smile. Then she turned back to Zach. "Okay, buddy. Let's see if we can gift-wrap a monster."

If you'd have asked Poppy two weeks ago how she'd feel about standing in the middle of a school carnival while two kids wound toilet paper around her…well, the answer would have been pointedly direct and most likely, dripping with sarcasm.

But now? She'd willingly say there was no place she'd rather be.

"Come on, guys. You can do it. You can mummy me better than that. Go crazy."

Zach and Zoe stepped up the pace.

"Go faster."

They began to run.

"Faster, faster! Go! Go! Go! Go!" Suddenly, Poppy's pocket began to buzz. But her arms were firmly swaddled to her sides. "Oh—will you get my phone?"

"Yeah." Zoe was closest to the pocket. She reached in and pulled the phone out, then took a look at the screen to check the text message. "It's Dad."

"Is he here?" Zach was slightly out of breath from running, but his voice was filled with excitement and joy.

"No." Zoe held the phone close to her face. "It says, 'tell the kids I'm sorry, but I can't make it'."

Poppy heard the faint sound of tears beginning to choke in Zoe's throat. Zach looked at his feet and stubbed at the gym floor with the toe of his sneakers.

They were crushed. And Poppy was crushed for them. "Oh. I'm sorry, guys."

Truthfully, Poppy was crushed for herself, too. She thought she'd gotten through to Ryan. All that honesty last night, and it hadn't mean anything to him.

From there, the party seemed joyless. The kids didn't want to Pin the Wart on the Witch's Nose or dance the Monster Mash. In fact, it seemed like all their happiness had been mashed out of them.

After school, they came home and went straight to their rooms. They did their homework without complaint. Zach didn't even protest when Poppy announced it was bath time—and when it was Zoe's turn, she didn't ask for bubbles.

Poppy ordered a pizza for dinner, but neither Zach nor Zoe finished a single slice. Zach picked at the pepperoni. Zoe mostly sipped on her glass of chocolate milk. Poppy didn't blame her. She'd like to drown her feelings about today in something, too.

Although Poppy hadn't heard from Ryan since the text Zoe had read at the party, all signs pointed to another late night for him. Surely, he'd have called or texted if he was going out for another dinner with Abigail after work?

Whatever the reason, Poppy couldn't handle the silence that surrounded the kids any longer. It was breaking her heart.

She decided a movie might get them out of their own thoughts. Maybe they could find a good Halloween flick with the On Demand feature on the TV box. It would be just the trick to pass the last little bit of the evening before bedtime rolled around.

Poppy put a bag of popcorn in the microwave and checked the list of available movies. When the microwave beeped, she dumped the fluffy kernels in a bowl and brought it over to the kids, where they lay flopped across two disparate parts of the living room sectional couch.

"Have you ever seen *The Creature from the Black Lagoon*? It's about a creature—from a lagoon!" Poppy sat in the corner of the sectional and tucked her legs up underneath her. "Or we can watch *The Wolfman*, which is basically a parable for how scary dads look when they don't shave."

Zoe stared at her feet so intently that Poppy thought the child's laser focus might sever a toe. Zach held on to his favorite stuffed monkey.

And no one made even the slightest move toward the popcorn.

"Okay, I know he didn't show up. But I bet he had a really good reason."

Zoe finally spoke up. "He only cares about work."

Poppy felt her own heart break at the sound of Zoe's words. These kids were hurting, deeply. Poppy remembered how it felt to have a preoccupied parent.

"That's not true," she said. She wanted to fix this mess. *But how?* "He loves you."

"He loves work more." Zoe reiterated her opinion on the subject.

"And he's good at it." Zach's implication was clear. Ryan wasn't good at being a parent.

Zach's words flipped on a light switch in Poppy's mind. Maybe there was a way to keep an evening like this from ever happening again in the Larson house.

"I think I just got an idea of how we can get his attention."

Zoe popped up from her burrow in the pillows. If nothing else, Poppy at least had Zoe's attention. That would be a start.

Poppy passed the bowl of popcorn to Zoe and beckoned Zach to follow as she headed to the stairs. "All right, you hold this. Bring it upstairs. Come on."

If all went well, Ryan would get the message soon. He wasn't the only one who could have conference room strategy sessions with colleagues. Poppy's colleagues were shorter, but she knew they were no less determined.

Chapter Six

RYAN DREADED WALKING IN THE house. He hadn't felt a sinking feeling like this since the last days of Laurie's life.

He knew there would be silence and looks. He'd be paying the piper in just a few short seconds, and he had no words to offer in his own defense.

Well, none that the kids would accept anyway. They didn't care about app interface meltdowns.

At the end of the main hallway, a small table from the upstairs playroom had been placed. In the left corner was a cup of pencils from Zoe's desk set. On the right side of the table, two glasses and a water pitcher had been placed. His old briefcase stood on the floor next to the little arrangement.

Behind the table stood Zach and Zoe. Zach wore his sweater and tie from Easter. Zoe looked very serious in a gray blazer and black skirt that would have made Abigail envious of the young girl's grasp of a power suit at such a young age.

"Hey guys," Ryan said skeptically. He didn't quite

know what to make of the whole tableau. But he figured he'd find out quickly. "What's all this?"

"Please have a seat." Zoe pointed at the small playroom chair, pulled up to the table. Otherwise, her face remained completely neutral.

Ryan first put down his briefcase and scarf in the kitchen, but then did as he was told. He sat down. Way down. He dwarfed the chair. At any other time, he would have laughed—but this was definitely not the time for mirth. "So...what's going on?"

Zoe glanced down at the teal-colored notecard she was holding in her hand. "That's what we would like to ask you."

"Okay. I know I missed the party." Ryan began to try and apologize. He said a quick, silent prayer that the right words to make amends would come to him. He needed all the help he could get right now. "Something came up at work and I—"

His daughter cut him off. "We're evaluating you in your capacity as 'father'."

Zach wrote a brief note on the clipboard in his left hand. "Shall we begin?"

The right words hadn't come to him, but Ryan opened his mouth again to speak anyway.

Zoe cleared her throat. She wasn't having any of his excuses. "Ahem. While my colleague and I feel it's clear that you love your children, your failure to meet them at their Halloween function—"

Ryan could feel it. His children—the little tiny babies he'd once held in his arms—were picking him up and throwing him under the bus. Hard. "Okay, well, you know, I got slammed and—"

"Please don't interrupt." Zoe raised a hand. "Your failure to show up, after you *promised* you would, is just one example in an alarming trend of how you choose to be a father. From our perspective, you care about work—"

Zoe tilted the notecard into Zach's field of vision so he could get a word in. "And your cell phone—"

"And your computer—" she continued.

Zach now read off a yellow notecard. The color changed, but the message remained the same. "And your cell phone—"

"And then, after all those other things, you care about your kids. When really, we should be first."

There it was. The gut punch. He'd been expecting it, but still, Ryan wasn't prepared for the tough reality Zoe had just laid down.

"Your priorities are out of…whark?" Zach stumbled over the note his sister held out for him.

Zoe whispered the correct term. "Whack."

Zach gave a quick head-bob as he corrected his error. "I mean, whack."

"Do you want to be the dad who breaks promises?" Zoe finally paused.

The silence fell heavily on Ryan.

He couldn't argue. He couldn't even offer a defense. Never had he been more proud of these kids in front of him. He was blown away by poise and maturity they showed in putting together this effort to force him to see how his actions affected them. Ryan didn't know how these amazing kids were his, but he did know one thing—he was truly blessed to be their father.

"No, I do not." Ryan shook his head and gave himself up to the mercy of the pint-sized court. "I don't."

"Then don't be," Zoe's voice held more than a proclamation. She offered a plea. "In summation, you should probably make more of an effort in the dad department. Do you agree with our assessment?"

There was only one answer. "Yes. Yes, I do."

"Here are the results of your evaluation. Please review."

Zach handed the clipboard across the table. Ryan reached out and took it. The lump reached his throat at the same time as a thin line of tears reached his lower eyelids.

The paper attached to the clipboard held a message.

There were four areas noted: reliability, focus, prioritization, team effort. Each word had a check in a box in front of it. Zoe had dotted each "i" with a heart.

Right below his marching orders, they'd written the title "Results."

The simple verdict was written in purple marker and decorated with green hearts: WE LOVE YOU!

Ryan had never sat through a more difficult assessment of his performance.

And he'd never been more grateful for a rating.

Zach and Zoe were great kids. They reflected the

best part of him. And they deserved the best part of him.

"I love you too." Ryan placed the clipboard on the table and stretched out his arms. "Get over here."

He curled Zach close with one arm. Zoe came to the other side and rested her cheek on his shoulder as they embraced.

They'd given him the greatest gift he could ever receive.

A second chance.

He looked at Poppy. Ryan knew that she had orchestrated this do-over with his kids.

"Thank you," he mouthed to her from across the room.

She smiled and nodded, then said something with a low whisper, almost to herself. Ryan thought he could make out the words, "I'm good at this…temporarily."

He decided that when October was over, he needed to talk to Poppy about taking on the nanny role permanently. The spark she'd brought to their house was good for all of them.

Rosewood Lane Farms had been providing pumpkins and fun to the families of the greater SeaTac area for more than fifty years. Ryan remembered coming out here as a child. It made his heart feel lighter to bring his own kids down this unpaved road for the same fun he'd once had.

And he had the woman next to him to thank for

making him draw a line in the sand—or the pumpkin patch dirt—and take a Saturday off to spend with his family.

The emails could wait. Mindful of the bullet point on *both* of Zach's notecards the other night, Ryan even left his phone back in the car.

"All right, gang," He swung Zoe's hand as they walked toward the pumpkins. "Since it's been brought to my attention that my priorities are 'out of whark,' let's see who can find the best pumpkin, huh?"

"Yes!" Zach bent his elbow and brought his fist down. A typical boy, he was always up for any challenge.

Zoe released Ryan's hand as she chased after her brother.

"Go for it, guys," Ryan shouted down the lane after the kids, almost certain they didn't hear anything their dear ol' dad said.

"I can't remember the last time I looked at pumpkins."

"Well, they're still orange." Poppy interjected her easy sense of humor. It flowed well with the lazy fall day.

Ryan took in the sight of the hay and the pumpkins scattered everywhere. It felt good to just stroll. He'd missed savoring the small things in life. "I've missed a lot lately."

"Well, you're here now."

"Thanks to you." He needed to be honest. It had taken a stranger to come into their lives and turn everything around for the better. "Just promise me you won't make me dress up for Halloween."

"Ooh, I make no promises. In fact, I could see you dressed as a smartphone. Like a really smart smartphone." A light twinkled in Poppy's eyes. They looked like the waters of the Pacific that flowed in to embrace Seattle. The perfect shade of Puget Sound blue.

Ryan knew he couldn't get caught staring into her eyes. Having to explain that would be even more difficult than the pint-sized inquisition from Zoe and Zach. "I take it you've got your costume."

"Are you kidding? I haven't missed a Halloween since I was two."

Somehow, he didn't doubt it. In fact, Ryan was surprised Poppy had missed the first two. "Hmmm…"

"Which was twenty years ago," she clarified.

"Right." Ryan played along, a beat late. As he'd realized the other night, his flirting game was way out of practice.

"I'm super young."

"Yeah, Zoe told me you were twenty-eight."

"Did she? Love her." Poppy laughed at the truth being revealed.

"I'm thirty-four; in case you were wondering."

"Oh, I wasn't—I Googled you."

She revealed that little bit of cyberstalking way too easily.

But in the spirit of honesty… "I Googled *you*."

"Well you had to. You're a techie. You Google

everyone." Poppy generously tried to let him off the hook.

Ryan drank in the blue of her eyes again. This time, he also noticed the thick brown fringe of lashes that framed Poppy's eyelids and the perfect curve of her eyebrows that anchored the top part of her face. He tugged his eyes downward, curving his gaze down the gentle slope of her petite nose and then traced the curves of her lips as they teased him with a smile.

Her face was as beautiful as her personality.

"Not everyone."

Ryan realized he wanted to get to know her better. He wanted to discover the secrets that a search on the World Wide Web could never reveal. But that wouldn't be fair to anyone in their little group. It would be unfair to Poppy—she came to their house looking for a job, not a romance. And if he acted on his thoughts, he'd probably scare her off. His kids deserved better than having to assimilate another new nanny just because their dad couldn't keep his thoughts from getting the better of him.

Two seconds of silence passed, then Ryan could tell Poppy had caught him staring. Immediately, she jumped over to a display of pumpkins of all shapes and sizes and shades. They were stacked on a lopsided pyramid of hay bales.

"Ooh, what about this one? For the front porch?" She pointed at a very round pumpkin with a yellow hue and a long, curved green stem.

Her choice was a classic pumpkin. But it wasn't

eye-catching enough for him. He'd left work behind to spend time with his family today, and they were going to get the best pumpkin Rosewood Lane could offer.

Ryan stepped back and pointed to a pumpkin just off to his right. Roughly the size of a microwave, it was the largest pumpkin anywhere in the vicinity. "Yeah, I kind of like that one."

Poppy's eyes went as round as the gourds all around. "Whoa. That one's like a pumpkin that ate a pumpkin."

"Hey, go big or go home."

"How much do you think it weighs?'

Usually, nerds never got the girl. They were punchlines, the nice guys who finished last. Not today. Something inside told him to pick up the pumpkin and impress Poppy. She definitely wasn't expecting it. "Listen, just because I'm a techie doesn't mean I can't lift a pumpkin."

His efforts made Poppy double over with laughter.

That really wasn't the effect Ryan was going for.

"I can't…" Ryan signaled defeat as he tried one last time to get a good grip on the back of the giant squash. Nope. "I can't lift the pumpkin."

Poppy swooped up to the other side. "Okay, I'm going to help you. I'm comin' in."

She leaned down and braced her hands on either side of the gourd. It didn't move even a centimeter. "Gosh, it's really heavy. I feel like you've got most of the weight on you."

"I think I do." Once they got it up, he carried it proudly. Maybe he could still impress her.

Or maybe he just needed to institute a corporate gym membership policy at Parcel Technologies. He would call his HR manager, Becky, the first thing on Monday and get that perk added to the team's benefits package.

"Ready?"

They sort of spider-crawled down the small hill and dumped the pumpkin in a waiting wheelbarrow. Ryan didn't care what this pumpkin wound up costing. It was coming home with them. Zoe and Zach would love having the largest jack-o'-lantern on the block. He couldn't wait to see the smiles on their faces when they saw the wheelbarrow's contents.

Just then, he heard a small giggle from over his shoulder. Zoe poked Zach as he pointed at Poppy. The kids had both seen everything, and they had huge smiles on their faces.

But something told Ryan their happiness had nothing to do with bringing home that pumpkin.

"Dad! Dad!" Zoe came running up behind Ryan, out of breath. "Did you know they have a kids' camp here?"

Ryan shook his head. "That must be something new."

"Can we stay for it, please?" Zach screeched to a stop in front of Ryan, causing a little cloud of dust to billow around his tennis shoes that lit up with every step.

"What is kids' camp?" Poppy asked. The two kids were almost too excited about the possibility to explain.

"It's a thing they're doing this afternoon with arts and crafts and a hay maze and face painting and games and pumpkin stuff." Zach's words came out so quickly, Poppy could barely keep up.

"Pumpkin stuff?"

The young boy nodded solemnly. "Pumpkin stuff. Like carving them and science experiments to make them blow up. And stuff."

"And stuff," Poppy reiterated. She turned to Ryan and gave a small shrug. "It does seem kind of fun."

"But what would we do while you all are doing… pumpkin stuff, guys?" Ryan asked the kids.

A staff member in an orange T-shirt and khaki shorts stopped as she heard Ryan's question. "We've got a restaurant back over there." She pointed to a barn-style building past the largest pumpkin patch. "Everything's set up nice in there. A lot of parents are making it a date day while the kids are occupied for a few hours. You should do that too, Mom and Dad."

Poppy almost lost her balance. She grabbed onto a scarecrow for support.

"That's not my mom," Zach explained. "That's our nanny. My mom doesn't even know we're here."

Poppy wondered whose face turned a brighter shade of red: hers or Ryan's.

"Their mom died. Several years ago. That's why she doesn't know what we're doing today." Ryan choked out the words. "Why don't you guys just go ahead and go? We'll go buy more pumpkins or something. Meet us back here at two, okay?"

The kids didn't even wave as they ran off, eager to join the fun.

The air still hadn't quite filled Poppy's lungs back all the way. She decided to straighten the scarecrow's hat. It seemed a lot easier than trying to talk.

"Did you see her face?" Ryan finally broke the silence.

"Nope," Poppy answered honestly. "All I saw was yours."

"Red?"

"Like Rudolph's nose."

"I guess I'm getting a jump on the Christmas season," he said, picking up a pie-sized pumpkin and putting it in the wheelbarrow.

Poppy waggled a finger. "Nope. One season at a time. Do not be the guy who starts buying Cadbury crème eggs before Valentine's Day has passed. Each holiday deserves to have special consideration."

"They do?"

A gentle fall breeze blew around them, shaking the straw that stuck out from the scarecrow. Poppy slicked her hands back across the front of her hair, trying to tame flyaway tendrils. "Absolutely. Wouldn't you want to feel special?"

"I guess I would. No one's asked me what I've wanted in a long time."

The sadness in his voice was unmistakable. Poppy's natural instinct was to help him turn his frown upside down. But something told her that cracking a joke or making a sarcastic comment wasn't the right response here.

"What do you want, Ryan?"

"I'd like my dreams back. I'd like to be a dreamer again."

Now Poppy felt even more confused. So far, she'd thought of Ryan solely as a high-tech workaholic. She wondered about this side she hadn't seen. But before she could ask, Poppy heard a low rumbling sound.

"Was that you?"

"It was," Ryan admitted. "So I guess what I'd really like is lunch. Do you want to go see what they have at that restaurant? It doesn't have to be a date."

Poppy didn't want to tell him that she'd prefer if it was.

She decided to keep that dream to herself.

The little restaurant in the barn was rustic, but charming. Strings of lights twinkled overhead. Flickering LED candles had been placed in the center of each table. Red and white checkered tablecloths added a farm-fresh feel and a dose of cheer.

It felt comfortable.

As Ryan pulled the chair out for Poppy, he thought

about how well that word fit. He also felt comfortable. For once, he felt at ease without his phone. He didn't feel like he needed to be plugged in. Why couldn't more days be like this?

The answer was more obvious than he cared to admit. He was the one keeping himself from having more days like this.

That needed to change. He needed more days where the kids got fresh air and he had a smile on his face. Ryan knew what he needed to do.

"I need to buy a sailboat," he said as he took the seat across from Poppy.

"Whaaat?" She extended the syllable by several beats.

"A sailboat. Don't you think the kids would love it?" He opened his menu and looked down. "Or maybe a camper. We could go up the coast, head into Canada. Explore a little bit. Do you think the kids would prefer sailing or camping?"

Poppy folded her hands on the edge of the table and eyed him carefully. "When do you plan to have time for all this recreation?"

Ryan studied her face. Skepticism was painted liberally over every plane and curve. "After the Food with Friends deal is through."

"So, once it's done, *you're* done? They're paying you enough so that you don't ever have to work again? That's awesome."

He'd given the wrong impression. "Well, no, not exactly. Although I won't deny that it will make a lot of things easier. It will pay off the house and pay for college for the kids. That frees me up to pursue other things I'd like to do."

Poppy lifted her water glass. "So what will you do?"

"Well, the team is already working on about three other apps."

"Ryan, that's not a camper or a sailboat." She gave him a level stare. "So once you finish this project, you're on to other projects?"

He'd stepped right into that trap.

"I'm a workaholic, aren't I?"

Poppy nodded way too fast for Ryan's comfort. "Totally."

"And you don't think the sailboat or the RV are good ideas?"

She squeezed a lemon wedge into her water before taking another sip. When Poppy put her glass down, she answered. "I think they're great ideas. I just don't think they're great for you."

That sounded damning, even though Ryan knew Poppy didn't mean it that way.

"Why not?" he asked.

"Because you need to make promises and stick with them. I know you're trying to do better. But painting a big picture of fun like that for the kids is going to get their hopes up. If the sailboat is just going to collect dust or barnacles or whatever at the marina, then it's not the right decision. You can rent one for the day. Or you can book a cabin in British Columbia for the weekend."

"You don't think I can change?" He could feel a hunger inside of him that had nothing to do with what he'd decided to order for lunch.

Poppy looked at Ryan thoughtfully. The fake flicker of the candle made a little spark twinkle around the edge of her irises.

"When your wife was alive, how did things around the house work?"

"I ran the office. She ran our home. She was a stay-at-home mom after the kids were born."

"And she was the planner, right?"

Ryan simply nodded, thinking of how much Poppy's ideas about holidays and Halloween and fall aligned with the type of joy and fun Laurie had tried to infuse throughout their lives.

Poppy paused, then continued. "And you were the dreamer. The guy with the ideas that made it all possible."

"That's certainly one way of putting it, yeah. We were a team." It felt a little strange talking about his wife with another woman, but somehow, he knew Poppy understood. Not only that, she didn't seem threatened by it.

Abigail had brought up his former wife and his family a few times and it always made the hair on his arms rise slightly. He hadn't been able to put his finger on the reason for that until this moment—but now he could see that Abigail's inquiries had been designed to stake out territory and make herself look like the woman who could do it all.

Ryan didn't want a woman who could do it all.

He wanted a woman who could turn his weaknesses into strengths. Someone who balanced out their home. Someone who understood they didn't have to replace what had once been in the Larson house, but could make the future brighter than a holiday full of twinkle lights.

If he was wading back into the dating pool, he needed to understand why he was doing it and what he hoped to get out of it—just like he'd do at work for a new project.

Ryan knew he needed to be careful. Poppy was right. The sailboat idea was just a thought. He couldn't make decisions on some kind of crazy whim that would affect his kids for the years to come. If he was going to date, he needed to be clear on his reasons why. And right now, he wasn't even clear on the who. Abigail was ready to date, and she'd made her interest clear. She was a nice, successful woman.

But was dating her what he truly wanted? Was he going out with her because he saw her fitting into the Larson family? Or would dating her be like buying a sailboat—an idea that seemed good on the surface, but completely impractical in reality?

In all honesty, Ryan didn't know. But he knew he needed to figure out what he wanted and why, and he needed to do it sooner rather than later.

Somehow, they wound up with twelve pumpkins.

Poppy didn't even know how that happened. Ryan walked through the Rosewood Lane patch like some sort of fairy godmother, granting pumpkin wishes to his kids. If they so much as pointed at a pumpkin, he tossed it in the wheelbarrow.

When they returned to the house, Ryan told Poppy she could have the rest of the afternoon off before coming back for a few hours tonight, but she was also welcome to stay and join him and the kids for an afternoon of carving. Zach and Zoe said "pleeeeeeaaaaaase" and made all sorts of sad eyes and puppy dog faces at her.

Little did they know, she would have stayed no matter what. They didn't have to beg. She loved making these memories with them.

And she loved seeing Ryan interact with them like the engaged father she knew he truly wanted to be. Seeing him live out his love for them...well, it was incredibly attractive.

Or, it would be incredibly attractive if he wasn't her boss.

But, he was. So, she couldn't think of him in any other way.

Except Ryan was attractive. That was the truth. And Poppy tried never to lie.

Zoe dug out the pulp from the oblong-shaped pumpkin she'd selected as they were about to leave the patch. She lifted a handful of strings and seeds to shoulder height and wrinkled her nose. "It feels squishy."

"Oh…like worms," Ryan teased as he grabbed a handful of pumpkin goop from his own jack-o'-lantern-in-progress.

"Dad, gross." Zoe tried to dodge the sludge Ryan waved close to the side of her face.

"Are you sure? I thought you loved eating worms." Ryan kept waving the pumpkin strings in Zoe's face. She batted his hands away with a girlish shriek before he could get it close to her mouth—but her dad tried anyway. "Get in there."

"Dad!"

There were only a few more pumpkins to finish up, and Poppy didn't want to run out of time to discuss the one remaining key to Halloween fun. "Okay, let's talk costumes. Time to get serious."

"All right." Ryan cut the shape of a mouth into the giant pumpkin he'd insisted on bringing home. While Zoe, Zach, and Poppy had all carved multiple pumpkins, Ryan had only tackled one.

Sure, it was the Titanic of pumpkins, but still…

Zoe answered Poppy with quick certainty. "I'm going to be a witch."

"Good witch? Or bad witch?" Poppy's mind began to spin. Costume ideas could go either way, but would be very different, depending on what Zoe chose.

"A good witch."

"Good luck with that," Ryan threw the teasing comment out under his breath.

Zoe returned fire, but instead of words, she used pumpkin guts. "Dad!"

Ryan ignored Zoe's ammunition and turned his attention to Zach. "What about you, buddy?"

"I'm going to be a spider."

"Really?" Ryan raised an eyebrow at his son's idea.

Like every older sister before her, Zoe jumped in with a reply before her younger brother could explain his reasoning. "Poppy says the best way to get over your fears is to face them."

"Well I couldn't agree more." Ryan's smile melted Poppy's heart like caramel ready to be poured over a juicy fall apple. "You're going to make a great spider, bud."

"I'm going to scare everybody." Zach's chest puffed with importance.

"Except for yourself," Poppy pointed out.

"Hey, actually, you know, there's a costume shop near where I work," Ryan said. "We could actually—"

Pffft. Poppy admired Ryan for trying, but really? No. Just no. "Costume shop? That's for amateurs. We're going to make our costumes."

Zoe nodded in agreement, a giant smile on her face.

"Really?" Ryan seemed like he couldn't believe what Poppy was biting off. Silly man, he had no idea.

When it came to Halloween, there was no easy button. Poppy had never bought a costume, and she wasn't about to start now. "Yeah. My sister does it every year."

Ryan rinsed pumpkin strings off his hands, then

stepped to dry them at the towel looped through the refrigerator handle. "Wow."

While he was out of earshot, Zoe leaned across the counter toward Poppy and lowered her voice. "Thanks for making our dad spend time with us."

Poppy couldn't take the credit away from Ryan. He'd taken the performance review to heart last night and immediately made a change. Poppy felt a great deal of admiration for Ryan. He'd been able to admit where he'd gone wrong. "Hey, I didn't make him do anything. You guys showed him what he's been missing."

"All right…" Ryan returned back to his giant pumpkin and picked up the knife for the finishing touches on the jack-o'-lantern's traditional-looking face.

Zach put the lid back on his pie-sized pumpkin. He'd carved a lopsided circle through the pumpkin flesh. It was possible that jack-o'-lanterns weren't quite his thing yet. "Hey, Dad?"

Ryan put the lid back on his own pumpkin and stepped back to admire the finished product. "Yeah?"

"After we're done carving pumpkins, can you make your special hamburgers?" Zach had been really quiet for the last few minutes. Poppy was proud of him for speaking up and asking for what he thought would make the family day even more fun.

"That's a great idea." Ryan began to put his watch back around his wrist. "You know, maybe Poppy can help with that."

Poppy nodded. She could help with anything the kids needed her to do, but she didn't understand why Ryan wouldn't want to do his own burgers. Wasn't grilling supposed to be a manly thing?

"You're going back to work?" All the afternoon's joy drained from Zoe's face. Poppy watched it slip away like the current racing down a river.

"I've got a dinner thing," Ryan mumbled, but everyone in the kitchen heard each syllable loud and clear.

"With Abigail?" Zoe practically spit out the name.

Ryan's head snapped around. Deep creases ran across his furrowed forehead. "Yeah. How did you—"

"Italian again?"

Whoa. Zoe's snark game was really on point. Her sarcasm sounded as though it came from a fully-fledged teenager.

Alarm bells went off. Poppy had to save this. How could Ryan not see that he was about to taint every single joyful memory that had been created today? When the kids looked back on this day, they'd always remember it as the day their dad spent *almost* the whole day with them, but then left anyway.

She would not let that happen. She would not let their trip to the pumpkin patch and the hours of carving be wasted. "Hey, why don't we go do dinner? How does pizza sound?"

"Really?" Zoe's voice begged Poppy to not let her down.

"Yeah. I know a great place downtown, and I think

the manager likes me, so we can get extra toppings." Poppy knew she was overselling it, but she felt like she needed to. Desperate times, desperate pizza topping measures.

Ryan gave his giant pumpkin a double tap on the stem. "All right, well…looks like you guys have things covered here. I'm going to go up and get ready."

Poppy couldn't even make eye contact with Ryan. How could he be so clueless? His kids needed him. A few minutes ago, she thought he'd gotten it. Now, Poppy saw she'd given him way too much credit.

"Okay." Zoe watched her dad as he headed up the stairs.

"All right, let's finish carving these pumpkins."

Zoe stabbed at her pumpkin with force. "I don't like this Abigail person."

"You can't dislike someone you've never met." Poppy wanted to agree with her, but she needed to be the grown up here.

Because Ryan sure isn't being one.

Poppy darted her eyes from Zach to Zoe. Had she said that out loud? Thankfully, both kids remained focused on their pumpkins. Poppy felt her blood pressure spike begin to recede.

Zoe continued inflicting her emotions on the hapless jack-o'-lantern. "I don't like Benedict Arnold, and I haven't met him."

Benedict Arnold? Although Zoe had been listening to the cast recording from a Lin-Manuel Miranda musical recently, Poppy had no idea what cloud Zoe had pulled this defense off of. "Good point. But he did live over 200 years ago. So, it would be hard for you to have actually met him. Besides, I'm not completely sure your analogy applies here."

"Maybe she's a traitor, like Benedict Arnold." Zoe clearly didn't care about rationality right now.

"Really, Zoe? Would your father be spending time with a traitor?" The shrug Zoe gave told Poppy that argument made no difference to her. "I'm sure Abigail is very nice. Because your dad is nice. And smart. And fun. And he wouldn't waste one piece of garlic bread on someone who wasn't."

This time, Zach spoke out. "But he's going to marry her and she's going to be our new mom."

"No… It's only their second date. A lot has to happen between date number two and 'let's get married'." Poppy thought she'd better address the elephant she suspected was dancing all around the room. "Besides, no one could ever replace your mom."

"But we don't like her." At least Zoe remained consistent in her opinion. No one would accuse her of being one of those wishy-washy kids.

Zach took his sister's assessment one step further. "Yeah. We like you."

"I like you guys too." Poppy sighed. They'd never know how much. "But you can like more than one person."

It was sort of how she knew she liked Ryan. But with Date Number Two with Abigail about to happen, there was no way she could ever tell the kids that little secret.

Poppy thought back to the afternoon at Rosewood Lane. They'd even had a lunch that had felt like a meal with a connection, although it wasn't a full-fledged date.

She could have sworn Ryan was treating her differently. Like he was interested or something.

But apparently not.

Poppy really needed to reassess all her skills associated with dating—because they were not working. At all. If only men were as easy to figure out as carving a pumpkin…

"You should marry our dad."

"Ha." Poppy almost choked on Zoe's proclamation. Was she an eleven-year-old mind reader? Definitely time to change the subject. "Who here likes pineapple pizza?"

"Our dad likes pineapple pizza."

Why did she keep bringing up her dad like that?

"You could have that at your wedding."

Poppy wanted to shout, but that wouldn't have helped matters. *Stop it, Zoe.*

"And gummy worms!" Zach chimed in. "You could have a gummy worm wedding cake!"

Oh my gosh. Him too? Poppy forced herself to close her jaw. It had never dropped like this before.

Alert. Alert. Redirect. Redirect. Laugh it off, Poppy. Laugh it off.

"You know who could perform the ceremony?"

She spun her jack-o'-lantern around and showed it off to both kids. "This guy!"

"Yeah!" Zoe clearly supported the idea.

"He'd be like, 'you may now kiss the bride!'" Poppy made kissing noises as the pumpkin chased Zach. He ducked and rolled, trying to avoid Poppy's silliness.

They were all laughing together, but on the inside, Poppy wasn't feeling very humorous.

Ryan couldn't even commit one full, uninterrupted day to his kids. He certainly wasn't going to be the kind of guy who could commit to her in the way she'd dreamed of since she was a girl.

About the time that she and the kids had the kitchen carving station cleaned up, Ryan came downstairs. He had on a gray sport coat, and Poppy could smell the definite scent of woodsy spruce a mile away. And was that hair gel? She did a double-take, but tried to be stealthy so he didn't see her checking him out.

He was taking Date Number Two seriously.

Ugh.

Looking at Ryan's dapper appearance confirmed to Poppy that she couldn't take any of the children's hopes and dreams seriously, lest she allow her heart to become as traitorous as Benedict Arnold. There were no pumpkins performing wedding ceremonies in her future.

Ryan kept his hands in his pockets as he and Abigail walked down a sidewalk in downtown Seattle on their way from the car to the restaurant. Abigail's arm swung gently at her side and Ryan had caught her periodically looking toward his hand.

This might be the second date, but Ryan wasn't there yet. He just couldn't reach out and hold her hand. Ryan didn't quite know why, but he wasn't feeling it at all. Maybe Zoe's prickly reaction earlier had rubbed off on him.

The sound of Abigail's designer heels tapped along the concrete. "Well, I'm glad you could make it out tonight."

"It's funny, I feel like I'm still getting used to the whole 'dating' thing." Ryan felt like he should offer some kind of explanation for his reticence.

"Yeah, the cologne tipped me off."

If she hadn't given a half-smile, Ryan would have taken the tone of her voice as criticism.

Ryan lifted the lapel of his sport coat and gave it a sniff. "Oh? Too much?"

Abigail threw her head back and laughed. Ryan thought the laugh was about as strong as the cologne— which was to say he knew she was trying too hard to make light of the situation.

"Maaaaybe a little," she said.

Clearly this evening was starting well.

"It'll dissipate by Halloween," Ryan promised. *Were his cheeks starting to flush?* That wasn't what a guy was supposed to do on a date. He had given so many pitches in so many boardrooms, and this—this—was what made him embarrassed?

Good grief. He wanted to revoke his own man card.

"Well, okay. I can wait." Abigail raised her palm and laughed, trying to blow the whole awkward moment off.

Ryan didn't know if he wanted to go into the restaurant or back to the car. "To be honest, I haven't really dated since my wife died."

It had never been like this with Laurie.

The only other woman he'd really spent unfiltered time around since Laurie died was Poppy. And come to think of it, it wasn't like this with her, either. Poppy made him laugh. She held his phone. She held a mirror up to the way his actions affected his children. She made him better.

And wasn't that what he'd told himself earlier today?

"You know, I think it's really great that you are getting back out there—especially with me. You don't even have to worry about making a good first impression because I'm already impressed." Abigail laid it all out.

Ryan wasn't quite sure what to say, but a mutual compliment seemed like a good plan. "Likewise."

"Well, look at us…impressing each other." The careful smile fell from her face. "You okay?"

"Oh, yeah. Yeah…" Ryan lied through his teeth.

Why couldn't he click with the idea that a pretty, smart woman was interested in him? She easily fit in his world. They both understood each other's 9-to-5 lives. But would she understand that part of him that came after he finished the day's work? Even though he worked many crazy hours these days, the one thing that would never change in Ryan's world was the simple fact that his kids were everything to him.

They deserved his total honesty. "Actually…my kids are a little worried that I'm dating again."

"They probably think I'm trying to replace their mom. You know, it's like in business. When one company takes over another, the employees are always worried they're going to be replaced with new staff."

"Yeah…" Ryan considered Abigail's merger analogy. Maybe she had more instinct where kids were concerned than he'd given her credit for. He'd probably written this evening off too soon. Maybe all the dust and the hay out there at Rosewood Lane had gotten to him.

It was easier to blame it on that than to think that Poppy had gotten to him. She was their nanny. As much as he wasn't sure Abigail was the one, Poppy wasn't either. She enjoyed his kids, but that didn't mean she wanted to adopt them. It just meant she had an open heart. She didn't want anything permanent—she couldn't even stay on at the job with them longer than a month. For him to act on anything he might begin to feel with anyone, he needed to know it was someone who could be around for the long haul.

Abigail continued talking and Ryan forced himself to put his attention back on her.

"I just don't think it has to be that way. We just

need to show Zoe and Zach nobody is being replaced. We're just making each other stronger."

From a business perspective, Abigail's logic made total sense. "I like the sound of that."

And that's exactly what he'd told himself today. He wanted someone to balance strengths and weaknesses with. Abigail's words were practically a sign that he needed to give this a shot.

Would the kids see it that way? As they walked into the restaurant, Ryan *almost* had himself convinced that they might.

Almost…but not quite.

When Ryan pulled up in the driveway, he saw Poppy sitting on the front step, surrounded by pumpkins. Candles glowed through their cut-out eyes and smiles.

The whole scene looked magical. Like a Halloween happily-ever-after.

"Hey." Ryan gave Poppy a wave as he stepped onto the front walk, admiring the day's handiwork. "Wow, these are award-winning."

He lowered himself onto the step near Poppy.

She gave him a half-laugh, but didn't say anything about the kids or the pumpkins, which surprised Ryan.

"How was your date?" she asked.

"Not exactly award-winning, but it was okay, I guess," Ryan summed up his evening with a shrug. Not for the first time tonight, he regretted not staying home instead—finishing the pumpkins and making those burgers Zach had requested.

"Oh!"

If Ryan didn't know better, he'd say the tone of Poppy's voice moved several points up the chipper scale from where it had been just moments before.

"But she wants to go out again, so that's… something." Just what, though, he didn't really know. He couldn't quite put his finger on Abigail's endgame. Did she like him for him? Or did she see it as some kind of personal-quasi-business relationship where they could be some kind of power couple, making tech deals all across Japan?

"That is something."

"Is it?" Ryan struggled. He wanted to feel like he was moving forward into the future. His business had finally taken off. Was it wrong to want his personal life to do the same?

Was it wrong to want to come home every Halloween to glowing jack-o'-lanterns, bat cookies, and smiling children wearing homemade costumes? He wanted his family back. A complete family.

Poppy put a smile that was two sizes too big across her face. "Yeah."

"Because I'm not sure the kids are going to like the idea."

"Oh, I think that's probably natural." Poppy echoed the same sentiment Abigail had earlier.

"Yeah." Ryan had hoped Poppy would expand on her thought and offer some ideas to help smooth that transition. She knew the kids so well. She would know what to do. But she didn't say anything further. "Well, thanks again," he said. "For…everything."

"You're welcome. For everything." The porch light caught the edge of that Puget Sound blue in Poppy's eyes.

She leaned to the right, getting closer to Ryan and tucked her head low, to where it was about to brush his shoulder.

He knew it. It wasn't just this porch that felt magical. It was the spark between them. He did see something flare in her eyes. There was something right here, right now. She felt it too.

Ryan knew he should have felt nervous about the contact that would happen in about one-point-two seconds, but instead, only relief washed through his veins. Only the good kind of adrenaline—the one that promised hyper-awareness and the ability to remember every detail—not the one that pulsed with fear.

Even though he'd tried to give it his best shot, Ryan had felt awkward all night long with Abigail. Nothing in him warmed to her beyond a business friendship. Surrounded by candles and pumpkins and porch light though, Ryan realized he felt completely warm. In fact, he identified very strongly with the flames dancing on the wick of each and every candle around him.

And it was all because of Poppy. This woman and her easy-going ways, her heart for his kids, and her ability to make anything—even picking up an oversized member of the squash family—fun.

Ryan leaned forward slightly. If he met her half way, maybe she'd understand everything inside without him saying a word. She had a knack for seeing things as they truly were—and making them better. She was the answer to all the questions he'd thought earlier in the barn at the pumpkin patch.

It wasn't Abigail. It was Poppy.

She made him better. She made him want to be a better father. And now, he realized he wanted to be a better man—for her.

Ryan's heart began to pound as he anticipated the embrace. He would slip his arm around her shoulder and pull her close.

And then she'd understand. And he'd understand. And it would be…well, magical.

Just as his hand almost brushed against hers, she pulled back.

All of the warmth and glow and magic sucked back like a tide before a tsunami. In an instant, it was all gone.

Poppy jangled a key ring between them. "Oh… I was getting my keys."

He'd gotten it all wrong. Ryan bit his tongue to keep from saying what he really wanted to. He couldn't believe he'd misread everything.

He couldn't believe that twinkle in her blue eyes wasn't really there to begin with.

"Sorry. I saw you going in for the lean…I thought you were…" Ryan made a back-and-forth gesture with his hands. "I thought we were…hugging."

"Hug?" Poppy clearly questioned Ryan's strategy. "That's what that was—a hug?"

Ryan mentally kicked himself. He didn't need to be back in the dating pool at all if he couldn't even pull off a simple hug. How had he ever gotten married in the first place? "Well, I—"

Poppy corrected his form. "It was more sort of hug-adjacent."

"Yeah. Which is okay. I mean, we're friends. Friends hug." He felt himself blowing out that flame inside that had glowed just moments before.

Friends.

Friends hug.

That's all he could ever be to Poppy. She was his kids' nanny, for goodness' sake. Hitting on the nanny—Ryan had just become every cliché in the single-dad book. Ugh.

"Yeah, Hugs with Friends. Another new app." Once again, Poppy made a joke and everything changed.

He wasn't sure it had changed for the better, but it had been a necessary change.

"There you go. I owe you again." He owed it to her to not be the guy who hit on his nanny. This was a business relationship. Wasn't he supposed to know how to operate in manager-employee scenarios? It was a good thing HR wasn't here.

Or the kids. Zoe and Zach would have been worse to deal with than HR. He never would have heard the end of it.

And this had to be the end of it. Poppy clearly

wanted it that way. She wasn't interested in Hugs with This Friend.

"Okay, I'm just getting my bag." This time, she was extra careful as she leaned to the side and lifted her bag off the porch step.

Ryan did an exaggerated lean back toward the column behind him. "I'll stay away."

Poppy stood and waved. "Bye, friend."

"Bye…friend."

Hugs with Friends. It could be a thing. Too bad Ryan realized he wanted more than just a hug from Poppy. He wanted the magic.

Chapter Seven

THE NEXT MORNING, OUT ON Megan's deck, Poppy raised her arms high for mountain pose, then lowered down for chair pose.

And hold...

Unfortunately, Megan wasn't interested in holding anything. She wanted to repeat the same question over and over. "Hugs with Friends?"

"It was the pinnacle of awkward." Poppy continued through the movement, dropping down to her cobalt-blue mat for snake pose.

"Well, did you hug him back?" Megan was like a Labrador retriever with a bone. And a stick. And a tennis ball.

Maybe if Poppy stated the truth emphatically, her sister would get it. "It wasn't romantic. It was a misunderstanding."

Or maybe not. "Well, everything happens for a reason."

"Would you not make this into something that it's not?" Poppy tried to roll her eyes, but the quick action made her dizzy as she pressed her palms into the earth and extended her spine.

Find the zen, Poppy. Don't let it get to you.

Poppy wished she knew exactly what *it* was— Megan's incessant questions or the fact that she had wanted that embrace with Ryan far more than she'd admit to herself. Or to Miss Matchmaker on the pink foam mat next to her.

"Because this is what you do, Poppy. You run when things get good."

Megan's statement hit below the belt. Well, below the stretchy yoga pant waistline.

"What if they're too good? That means they might end badly." The fear overtook all of Poppy's careful attempts to avoid speaking the truth.

"No, it doesn't have to." Megan contradicted the anxious little voice in Poppy's head that wouldn't shut up.

Poppy bent one knee and stretched the other back, then raised her hands into Warrior One pose. Her body felt in perfect balance.

Her mind did not.

"See, this is complicated, Meg. It's not just about me. Zach and Zoe want me to marry their dad. It's not fair for them to think something might happen between Ryan and I when it can't."

Megan brought herself back to center, then sank back into a chair pose. She didn't miss a beat of the yoga sequence or of the line of questioning. "And why can't it, exactly?"

Poppy wanted to say "duh," but that seemed childish. "He's my boss."

"Temporarily," Megan reminded.

"He's on date number two with Abigail, and date number three is pending."

Megan tapped her teeth with her tongue. "Oh."

"And he asked me for dating advice." Back to snake pose.

Megan brought herself back to center once again and then leveled with Poppy. "You know I couldn't ask for a better sister."

"But?" A catch was coming, Poppy could feel it. So much for a quick, stress-free outdoor yoga session to help her find that elusive state of contentment this morning.

"You've been here for me and the kids, and I appreciate every minute. Every dragon pillow fight and mac n' cheese."

Poppy took in a deep breath of the chilly fall air, then exhaled deeply with full use of her diaphragm. Good yoga technique was helping her stall for a second, and that, at least, filled her with a momentary bit of gratitude.

"Where are you going with this?" Megan was laying it on thick. The hairs on the back of Poppy's neck began to stand due to suspicion.

"You committed to us, but we can't be the only commitment you make."

Was Megan saying Poppy had failed at what she'd set out to do? It wasn't her fault that she'd needed to go in a different direction. She'd been so close to letting her heart commit fully to the Larson family—each one of them—and then it had backfired terribly. No one could possibly blame her for wanting to get away from that situation.

Right?

That's what it was. Poppy wasn't failing at commitment. She was succeeding at protecting her heart.

Poppy twitched her top lip as she tried to convince herself that her position on the matter was correct. If her sister wanted commitment, they'd start with seeing how committed she was to holding her chair pose.

"Go down a little lower. Lower. Lower. Lower."

With each notch downward, Megan got a little more wobbly. Poppy pressed her toes to the mat and grounded herself.

Steady, Poppy, steady. She wasn't just silently coaching herself through holding the pose. She was reminding herself not to let her sister get to her or fill her head with nonsense about things that could never come to pass. The one man she wanted to share a plate of antipasto with had asked her for advice on dating another woman.

Poppy wasn't crazy. She actually was the very opposite. The calendar would turn to November soon, and things would change for Ryan—his project would be over, he wouldn't need a nanny any longer, and he'd be free to pursue Abigail without the chaos of his current schedule. Poppy refused to waste her time pining for something she could never have. Poppy's goal with this foray into commitment was to prove she could do adult things.

Well, walking away from someone who didn't want her in the same way she wanted him was the height of maturity. She didn't like it, but she would do it with grace, and on her own terms.

And that was really all Poppy could ask for.

More or less.

Megan shifted her weight and collapsed onto the mat.

"Good," Poppy said with half a laugh, as Megan reached out and gave Poppy a shove. Poppy toppled over.

She'd almost fallen last night, too. She needed to figure out how to stand. The end of October—and the end of her commitment to the Larsons—was coming. She'd save herself a lot of heartache if she could just remain standing.

Halloween was just around the corner. Ryan dug out some old decorations from the attic and decided to put them up around the kitchen and living room while the kids got ready for school.

They'd be shocked when they realized their old man could do holiday stuff, too.

He had the music-streaming app set to a Halloween-themed station and all the crazy songs he remembered from his own childhood played one after the other.

Ryan was so into his decorating that he didn't hear the click of the front door as Poppy came in.

"This is awesome." Her enthusiasm brightened an already festive morning.

Ryan taped a banner reading "Trick or Treat" in place over the stove. "Glad you approve."

"I do!"

After last night's adjacent-hug, Ryan had thought he'd never hear those two words out of Poppy's mouth. But…moving on…

"Question…do you think we need more decorations?" He asked, but already knew the answer.

"Absolutely. But then you'd need a bigger house." She took off her jacket and looked around the room. "Where are the young'uns?"

"They're upstairs, brushing their teeth."

Poppy looked down at the candy dish on the kitchen counter. She picked up the last few remaining pieces, likely remembering that the dish had been much more full when she'd left last night. "You didn't."

"What?" Ryan brought two mugs of coffee with him as he strolled across the kitchen.

Poppy sounded scandalized. "Candy for breakfast?"

She was cute when she sounded scandalized. Her nose wrinkled just a bit and her smile pushed her cheeks up to lift the corners of her eyes.

"Eh, it was just one little piece." He sat one mug down in front of her. "Cream…two sugars?"

She smiled and gestured at his mug. "Black, one sugar."

So she'd been paying attention to his preferences, too. That was nice. They clinked their mugs together.

Everything about this moment seemed domestic. Perfect, even. As if it was what had been missing from the heart of this home for so many years. Coffee, the sound of kids getting ready for school, jokes, a favorite song on the radio... "If somebody came in here and saw us, they'd think we were some old married couple."

"Old?" Poppy questioned only one detail of Ryan's scenario.

He'd once hoped to grow old with someone. He'd still like that chance. "Super old."

"How many decades have we been together?"

"Three. We met—"

Poppy jumped in to add her own details to the story. "On a blind date."

"On a blind date, yes." Technically, they had been introduced by her sister, Ryan thought as he nodded in agreement.

"I thought you'd be horrible. But you weren't."

Ryan remembered her summation of dates that started with antipasto. At least he'd passed the test in this imaginary scenario. "I was witty and charming."

She shook her head and waved her pointer finger. "No, that was me."

"Right. Now I remember. Your jumping jack routine was perfection."

Poppy stifled a giggle. "As I said, I like to work out wherever I can. You can't always do a full yoga session."

Now it was Ryan's turn to laugh. Poppy continued. Clearly, she was on a roll. "We had a small wedding."

"We had a big wedding." As much as she loved decorating and parties, Ryan knew nothing small would do for Poppy on her wedding day. "And we honeymooned at…Niagara Falls."

"No, see—you thought it was Niagara Falls, but that's just because the toilet overflowed in the airport hotel when our flight was cancelled."

Leave it to Poppy to keep his imagination from getting too serious.

"I remember now, yes. Instead, we stayed up the whole night, just listening to music." He took three steps back and turned up the volume on the speaker at the back of the room. "I do believe they're playing our song."

The Halloween classic, "Spooky," began to play.

"What a coincidence."

"What do you say?" Ryan stepped to the dining room and held out his hand. The idea to reach for Poppy just came to him, but he was certain it would go down as one of his best ideas ever. Maybe even better than Food with Friends.

Spooky Dances with Poppy. A limited-edition feature. No high-tech here. Just that most time-honored of all ways to connect a guy and a girl. Dancing.

"One dance?" he asked. "For old times' sake?"

"How can I say no to that?" Poppy crossed the hardwood floor and took Ryan's hand.

"You can't."

He tugged and spun her to exactly where he'd wanted her since they'd been sitting on the porch last night. Right into his arms.

"Oh!" She laughed, then spun again.

Finally, they were only a breath apart, holding hands and swaying to the jangly beat. Ryan pulled her just a little closer. Poppy looked up and shifted her hand to Ryan's shoulder. He could feel the outlines of her fingers through the lightweight wool of his sweater.

He relocated his left hand to rest lightly on her hip. The look on her face said she didn't quite know what was going on. Ryan didn't either, but nothing about it felt spooky. It felt right.

This was his Halloween prize. No tricks, only a treat. He'd tossed and turned all last night thinking about the missed hug.

The real thing was even better than the fragments of dreams.

They moved in time to the music, then Ryan leaned forward and dipped Poppy low. She giggled with surprise.

If Ryan moved his head just slightly, he realized he could kiss her.

He realized he *would* kiss her. Would she kiss him back? Or turn her head and make them wind up kiss-adjacent?

"Poppy! Guess what? Dad said he's going to take us trick-or-treating on Halloween!" The kids ran down the stairs with a shout. When they reached the first floor, neither seemed surprised to see Poppy flipping out of his arms and standing straight up.

In fact, they seemed strangely pleased. If he didn't know better, he'd say Zoe just winked at her brother.

The kids weren't fazed by the sight at all. He'd been worried for nothing.

"Nice try. I said Poppy will take you trick-or-treating, and I'll try to get there at the end," Ryan set the record straight.

"What time is the end again?" Zoe wasn't backing down without a little bit of pre-teen fight.

"Well, whenever you guys are done and eating candy. And by the way, you'd better save me some." Ryan could still smell the faint whiff of gardenia perfume. Poppy stayed close.

Even more than a fun-sized candy bar though, Ryan wanted Poppy to save him another place on her dance card.

"Oh, we make no promises." She looked up at him with a knowing smile. "But we are making…"

Poppy ran to the chair where two large purple bags had been placed beneath her jacket.

Zoe squealed. "Our costumes!"

Zach's face lit with excitement.

"We're going to finish them today," Poppy assured the kids.

"Whoa. Impressive." Ryan wondered what he'd done to deserve this woman in their lives.

Zoe pulled out a length of black velvet material. Sprinkled across the top were purple glitter stars.

"Poppy said she's going to make these costumes really special for us."

"I figure they haven't really done Halloween in a couple of years, so it was time to do it right." Poppy's face was lit up almost as much as the children's faces were.

He hoped that a little of it was due to their dance. He didn't really want to be shown up by a bag of craft-store goodies.

"Go home or go big, right?" She bit her lip. "Is that right?"

"Eh, it's close enough. All right, guys. Time for school." An idea came to him. He had a few minutes to spare this morning, and he wanted to make this sense of closeness last. "Hey, why don't we walk today?"

"But aren't you going to be late for work?" Zoe's jaw dropped.

"No. I'm confronting my fears, too." Poppy had been good for all of them. "Go on—go get your bags."

"Race ya." Zoe hit the ground running.

Zach lodged a protest. "No fair, you got a head start."

Ryan had gotten a bit of a head start this morning too. A head start on what he hoped might be the foundation of a future with Poppy.

But how could he tell her? He really didn't want to be that guy who made a move on the nanny. He decided that was a fear he'd need to figure out how to confront. And soon. Ryan knew Megan's husband would be back from deployment before Christmas. Surely when he returned, Poppy would be moving on.

When they stepped out on the porch, Zach did a quick zig-zag from the right side of the porch to the left side. Poppy reached back to grab his hand, but instead found Ryan's.

He wasn't complaining.

Ryan gave it a little squeeze, and Poppy shot him an expression of mock surprise. Ryan laughed at her, even though he hated that she also let go.

Poppy put her other hand out for Zach, and Ryan took Zoe by the hand. His heart melted as his little girl skipped down the street beside him.

He'd put so much time and effort into an app to connect strangers at the touch of a button.

But the connection he saw all around him came from the heart. It wasn't social media.

It was *family*.

Poppy pulled up in the traffic circle in front of Mercer Elementary. The afternoon routine had started to feel like second nature. She enjoyed getting to spend time with the kids once school had let out. She liked hearing about their day, what they'd learned. It was an unexpected perk of the job.

The kids climbed in the car and immediately started chattering over one another.

"Shhh…" Poppy said, placing one finger over her lips. Immediately, Zoe and Zach stopped.

Poppy wanted to pat herself on the back. Getting two kids to stop talking on the first try was kind of like finding a unicorn in your front yard.

"What is it?" Zach asked.

"I made more cookies today."

Zoe clapped. "Awesome. Can we have them for a snack?"

Poppy shook her head. "I thought we could do something even cooler. Why don't we take some to your dad's office? I made up a plate for the breakroom and a special bag for your dad."

"We never get to go to Dad's office," Zoe said as she leaned forward slightly.

"Why not?"

Poppy looked in the rearview mirror and watched as the little girl gave a shrug. "Dunno. He's just always busy. And none of our nannies have been cool like you. They all made us just go home and do homework or flash cards."

"Well, flash cards are important. And you'll have to finish your homework as soon as we get back to the house. But I thought we could spread a little cheer first. What do you say?"

The reaction from the back seat of the convertible left no doubt that the kids supported the plan. Poppy tapped a few times on the screen of her phone and pulled up the navigation app. Setting the course for Parcel Technologies, she pulled away from the school and out to begin their journey.

It didn't take as long as Poppy had thought it would

to reach the downtown office. The afternoon traffic had been light. If they didn't overstay their welcome, they could get back on the road before the rush hour mess started up.

After parallel parking like a champ, Poppy mentally patted herself on the back, then asked the kids to stand on the sidewalk while she came around to the passenger side and picked up the cookies.

"There it is!" Zoe pointed to a window several floors up in a red brick building. "That's the Parcel Technologies logo!"

"Then we're in the right place. Let's go spread some Halloween joy!"

She wanted to do this for the kids, but also, Poppy had come up with this idea earlier because she'd decided to see where Ryan spent so much of his time.

And she wondered if she could catch a glimpse of Benedict Abigail Arnold on her own turf.

Not that Poppy was stalking.

It wasn't that at all.

It was just information gathering. If Abigail was going to become part of the kids' lives, then Poppy needed to know how to help the kids get over their fears of having their dad date this woman who they instinctively didn't trust.

They went inside the lobby. An exposed brick wall made the area look cozy. Zach punched all the buttons on the elevator. Luckily, the Parcel Technologies office was on the fourth floor. They wouldn't have to ride all the way to the top, stopping at every floor.

When they stepped off the elevator, Poppy couldn't help but look around. Everything was so shiny and clean. Glass walls were everywhere—and it seemed like there wasn't a single finger print on any of them. The bamboo floors reflected light and made everything bright. The office looked professional and modern.

She adjusted her jaw a little bit so that it didn't drop too far.

Ryan had built all of this. According to her Google research on him, he'd started this company from his college dorm room while he worked on his engineering degree.

She couldn't believe someone in their early twenties could have laid the groundwork for all this. In her early twenties, Poppy had tried to be an actress, a waitress, and a florist. The operative word in all of that was "tried."

Ryan had succeeded. And she realized it was hard to fault him too much for spending time on his work when the fruits of his labor were evident all around them.

"Dad!" Zach saw Ryan at the end of the hall and took off running.

"Shhh!" Poppy said again. This time, neither kid listened. Maybe her superpowers weren't quite so super, after all.

Zoe took off after Zach and they both wound up in their dad's office in a matter of seconds. Poppy felt a great wave of relief when she realized that Ryan wasn't on a conference call or in a meeting.

She opened the heavy glass door and wiggled her fingers in a playful wave. "Hey there."

The smile on Ryan's face was contagious. As soon as he lit up, the kids went to another level. Poppy felt the glow in her heart. You couldn't ignore the happiness inside the office.

"What are you guys doing here?" He opened his arms as he swiveled his chair so both kids had room to launch into him and give a full-body hug.

"We brought you cookies!" Zoe pointed back at Poppy.

"I did way too much baking today. You've got a breakroom, right?" She cast a glance at the bounty she had precariously balanced on one forearm.

"Absolutely. And hungry engineers everywhere. Young tech guys can't get enough of free food. Especially homemade free food. Sit it down on that table by the window and I'll have Jean come get it."

Poppy did as Ryan requested, then dropped a smaller orange bag on his desk. "This is your stash."

"Thanks."

For the first time, Poppy really studied Ryan's eyes. They weren't quite brown. They weren't quite hazel. They weren't quite chestnut. They reminded her of corduroy. Dark, comfortable, dependable.

Her fashion taste had always been a little too colorful and eclectic for anything as sturdy and timeless as corduroy, but as of right now, she made a vow to incorporate it into her wardrobe this fall.

Suddenly, it was her favorite.

The kids visited with Ryan and he showed them some slides from his upcoming presentation. Poppy could tell they didn't understand the technical aspects of it, but they felt a greater connection to what was taking place.

They could see for themselves what their dad had been putting in so many hours on.

For the first time, it had become real to them. Zoe tapped the screen and asked Ryan questions. Zach picked up the phone and the tablet on Ryan's desk and compared the versions of the app.

"They're the same!" he declared.

Ryan smiled. "Exactly. Everything's working just as it should."

And it wasn't just the app. Ryan was balancing the role of working dad just how he should. Poppy knew the kids would be better able to support their dad and his presentation now that they'd seen it firsthand. Bringing them here made Poppy feel like she'd made her own meaningful contribution. She couldn't speak Japanese like Abigail, but she could speak Zach and Zoe's language, and she knew this field trip would go a long way with them.

A tap on the door distracted everyone from the moment.

"Hey, Jean," Ryan said. He gestured at the tall woman with a beautiful cocoa complexion beneath short curls. "Poppy, this is my assistant, Jean. Jean, this is our new nanny, Poppy."

"It's nice to meet you, Poppy." The older woman

smiled. "Ryan, I've got Damian from TechWorks on line one for you, and Ms. Morwell would like to meet for a few more minutes as well."

Poppy hoped no one noticed the involuntary curl of her upper lip at the mention of Abigail's request.

"I thought Abigail had everything she needed for today?"

Jean shook her head. "She said she was making edits to your talking points and needs to get clearance from you on some changes."

Ryan sighed. "It never ends."

Poppy tried to reassure him. "It will at the end of the month, right? The presentation and all the changes and the last-minute meetings should be done then."

"I hope so," he said.

She didn't have any skin in this particular game, but Poppy couldn't keep her mind from repeating Ryan's assertion. She hoped so too. She hoped that at the end of the month, Abigail could hop on a plane to Japan and leave Ryan—wait...the kids, Poppy corrected herself—alone.

Abigail was waiting in Ryan's office after he walked Poppy and the kids back to the car. She already had the presentation pulled up on her laptop, ready to make some more edits. They'd spent most of the day holed up in the office changing slides and revising the talking points. Ryan thought his brain might turn to oatmeal or pumpkin guts or something.

As soon as he settled himself in his seat, she started in with her notes. "The people attending are not tech-savvy, so you're going to need to keep your geek-speak to a minimum."

"Is this your coded way of telling me to not talk about coding?"

"It wasn't exactly coded." She scooted the black leather chair on wheels ever-so-slightly closer to Ryan.

"Ha, ha. I will minimize my inner geek for the presentation." Ryan hoped he could keep his promise. Sometimes, he got so excited about this technology that he wanted to highlight every little detail.

But then, as this morning had shown him, sometimes, it was better to just go with the flow.

"Good." Abigail flicked her red pen between her fingers. "Have you ever been to Tokyo?"

"I barely have time to come here."

"Well, after the presentation—which Higashimoto will love—we should go."

"To Tokyo?" There was no such thing as the Single Dad Travel Agency. Going to Tokyo for work would be a challenge of epic logistical proportions. And going for fun wasn't on his radar because it wasn't on the kids' radar.

"Yeah. Take the corporate jet, meet everyone. It's an amazing city—just like New York. No one ever sleeps." It took a second for Ryan to realize that Abigail was serious.

She talked about Zoe and Zach like she knew them—picking up their photo off his desk, sharing about how to get them comfortable with Ryan dating again—but clearly, she had no life experience with parenting. A city so busy and chaotic that it never slept was the last place he wanted to take his kids. And a place where his kids wouldn't be comfortable was the last place he wanted to be.

On that note, he had two little people at home waiting on him. And one nanny. Ryan looked down at his watch.

"Got something on your schedule I don't know about?" Abigail's tone reminded Ryan of a porcupine. It got bristly very fast.

"I promised the kids I'd be home before dark."

Abigail tried to make a joke. "Hmmm…or you'll turn into a pumpkin?"

Little did she know he'd been surrounded by pumpkins lately. And loving every minute of it. "There were pumpkins involved."

Abigail's cell phone began to ring. She looked at the number on the screen and answered in Japanese.

Ryan turned in his chair and looked out the window at the afternoon sun.

He wondered what the word for "pumpkin" was in Japanese.

Ryan was late. But Poppy had brought the kids outside anyway. They'd have some fun and play until he arrived.

She tried to keep all nagging thoughts about how

he'd no-showed for the Halloweek party out of her mind.

Ryan had changed. She'd seen it. He was more engaged with the kids. He was carving pumpkins, walking them to school, feeding them candy for breakfast...

And pulling her close in the living room, dipping and twirling her as they danced.

Then he'd leaned close enough to kiss.

Those thoughts chased through her mind, too. But Poppy didn't want to keep them away. She wanted to relive them. Over and over and over...

It was as close as she'd ever get to any kind of romance with Ryan.

Zoe brought a football out of the garage. "Game on!" she called.

Poppy liked the idea of a diversion. She sprinted toward the lawn ahead of the kids. She wasn't quite sure how they'd manage a football game in the middle of all the yard décor, but she certainly planned to give it her best try.

"The goal's back there!" Poppy shouted and pointed at a tree on the other side of the fake graveyard.

Zoe ran right. Zach ran left. Poppy called after them. "Whew! Get it! Bring it here—bring it here!"

"Poppy!" Zoe threw a wobbly pass from the corner of the lawn.

Zach ran at full speed toward Poppy, but she caught the pass with ease. Being guarded by a second-grader wasn't much of a challenge. "Yeah, got it! Woo-hoo!"

Poppy broke into an improvised celebration dance on the lawn.

Ryan pulled his Jeep onto the street and observed Poppy's shimmy as he got out of the car. "It's looking like a pretty serious game you guys have got."

Poppy noticed him slipping his phone in the pocket of his sport coat. Her heart leaped. He was all theirs for the remainder of the afternoon. No distractions. Just family time.

She paused. Too bad they weren't actually her family.

"Dad! You're here!" Zoe ran straight for the sidewalk at a pace that would show up even an Olympic sprinter.

"Well, listen—it's not a real football game until the quarterback shows up." Ryan gave the perfect smug laugh as he gave his daughter a hug.

Poppy walked in a half-circle, keeping her eyes on the new athlete on the lawn. "Oh yeah? When does he get here?"

"Hey…that's enough outta you." He walked over toward Poppy and pointed at her. She half-expected him to lean in and hug her, too. She more than half-expected herself to hug back.

Just like this morning over coffee, if anyone saw them now, they'd think she and Ryan were an old married couple. Poppy decided she liked it that way. More than anything, it made her feel grounded. Committed.

Ryan affectionately rubbed Zach's head with an open palm. "What do you think—guys versus girls?"

He took off his sport coat and laid it on top of a pumpkin by the front tree.

"You are so on." Poppy and Zoe came together for a fist-bump.

Poppy hoped this wasn't flag football. When it came to playing with Ryan Larson, she'd prefer tackle football.

And she'd prefer playing for keeps.

Zach went in motion. He passed the football—to his dad. "Hut!"

Poppy ran between Zach and Ryan, trying to block the throw. Zoe called to her teammate. "Come on! Over here!"

"No—no—no!" Poppy squealed as Ryan went back in the shotgun to throw.

The ball arced seamlessly above her outstretched hands. Zach caught it with perfect form and ran it straight into the mock graveyard on the other side of the driveway.

"Yes! Touchdown!" Ryan did his own victory dance.

Poppy grabbed the football and set another play into motion. "Whoa! Slam!"

Zoe passed it back to Poppy with a little sneak and fade around Zach's left side. Poppy was concentrating so much on the neon orange football that she neglected to notice Ryan coming alongside her.

Ryan threw his arms around her waist. Suddenly, he was much more than hug-adjacent, tackling her into the pile of leaves below.

The game stopped. The kids went silent.

For a moment, the world stopped.

Ryan's face lingered just inches above hers. Poppy looked in his eyes and saw her own feelings mirrored in them. This wasn't Football with Friends—and neither of them wanted it to be.

The smallest little shift would bring them close enough to—*wait*—Poppy wasn't ready for that. Not here in front of the kids. She wanted to know what it was like to kiss this amazing man, but she wanted it to be *their* moment, far away from two pairs of very intuitive eyes. A little distance would provide a safety net for those amazing kids so they wouldn't get hurt if the kiss didn't go well.

She wriggled her left arm from underneath Ryan. "Uh-oh!"

"What?"

He rolled to the side just enough to give her the leverage she needed. Poppy brought her arm back and stretched like she was back home working on a yoga pose.

"Touchdown!" Poppy yelled, laughing and raising the ball high above her head.

Zoe's mouth and eyes went wide. She began to race toward Poppy and Ryan. "Coming in!"

Zach followed, leaping into the dogpile and landing on top of his dad. "What are you tackling me for? We're on the same team!"

For one moment, everything was fall and leaves and football and laughter. Kids were tickled. Memories were made.

Life felt perfect.

And then a car pulled into the driveway. Poppy recognized Abigail Morwell immediately.

Poppy's heart plummeted as though a goblin had popped up in front of her.

"Yoo-hoo!" the consultant said as she got out of her sleek, silver German luxury car.

Ryan rolled on his side and raised to an elbow. It took him a moment to say anything. Poppy felt certain Ryan hadn't invited Abigail here. Her appearance seemed to startle Ryan as much as it had shaken Poppy.

"Uh… Everyone, this is Abigail."

The four of them stood up and began brushing off grass and picking leaves out of their hair. Poppy stuck a smile on her face. The moment she'd loved so much had just evaporated into the crisp air. But there was no way she'd let this tall woman in the ivory trench coat and gauzy teal scarf know what she was thinking.

Poppy resolved to find some fake zen and wear it like a suit of armor. She was not about to let Abigail see Poppy's heart retreating to a private place before it broke entirely.

"Abigail, these are my kids." Ryan placed a hand on the outside shoulders of each child.

"Well, Zoe and Zach, right? It is so lovely to meet you both." Abigail greeted them formally. Poppy wondered if she'd start speaking Japanese or pull out some kind of presentation binder.

"And this is Poppy, my—I mean, our—"

Poppy needed the artificial zen now. She spat out the word. "Nanny."

"Nanny." Ryan hesitated before he parroted Poppy's answer.

"Nice to meet you, Abigail."

"Likewise." Abigail nodded, then turned her attention directly to Ryan. "The foreign analytics came in. I thought you'd want them—you didn't answer your phone."

"Yeah, sorry. I was going for a two-point conversion." Ryan gestured at the makeshift football field behind them, strewn with gold and brown and orange leaves. The football itself rested next to a pumpkin.

Alone. Just like how Poppy now felt.

Zach spoke up to sing her praises. It brought some cheer back to her heart. "Poppy scored three touchdowns."

"Two touchdowns. That last one does not count." Ryan raised his eyebrows as he protested.

Abigail had taken Poppy's picturesque family afternoon away. Poppy wasn't going to allow herself to be robbed of anything further—certainly not her hard-earned points on their football field. "Of course it counts."

"No way. No." Ryan made a gesture with his hands, like an umpire declaring a runner out. Wrong sport. But did it really matter?

"We'll talk about it later," Poppy said through clenched teeth.

"Okay. I've got to get back to work anyway, so…" Ryan brushed off the last of the crushed leaves, then paused. "You know, we could work here."

Poppy could see smiles on the kids' faces. They were just glad to have their dad under the same roof. On the other hand, Poppy would have preferred Ryan to leave, rather than be forced to accept this package deal of Abigail staying.

"Oh. I suppose—" Abigail sounded unsure.

Poppy could tell this wasn't how the other woman saw her unexpected interruption going. She'd probably thought she could just swoop in and carry Ryan off in her fancy sports car for another antipasto evening.

"Then we could have dinner, and you know—we're making pumpkin pasta. Pumpkin soup. Pumpkin pie. Pretty much anything pumpkin, right? I mean, if that's okay with you?"

Ryan's over-the-top sell of their evening made Poppy cringe. But she played along. It was best for the kids that they saw her getting along with Abigail. "The more the merrier!"

"Thank you, Poppy. All right." The smile on Abigail's face was completely forced. Clearly she could tell that she didn't fit here—but she wasn't giving up. Poppy could almost respect that determination, if it wasn't so aggravating.

"All right. Good game, good game!" Ryan gave Zoe a tight hug around the shoulders, then headed inside. Abigail followed quickly behind them.

"It was fun, Dad." Zach trailed in his dad's wake, trying to squeeze out what was left of the moment.

The talk turned to business before Ryan and Abigail even made it to the door. "Okay, so, what's the latest—" Poppy heard Ryan ask.

And just like that, the magic was over. Poppy stood alone in the front yard, wanting to dig a hole under one of the fake headstones so she could just crawl on in and die of some kind of very un-zen embarrassment.

Chapter Eight

ABIGAIL DIDN'T SEEM TOO IMPRESSED with the glow-in-the-dark skeleton that the kids had hung behind the desk in Ryan's home office. She made a few little quips about the decorations and then sat down at the laptop.

It seemed like Halloween wasn't her thing.

Ryan remembered an adage his grandmother used to quote when he was younger—that all work and no play would make one dull.

It wasn't that Abigail was dull. She was intelligent, poised, and at the top of her career. But she never slowed down. And other than their two evenings out, he'd never heard her talk about anything personal. No hobbies, no friends, no family stories—nothing.

When he compared Abigail to Poppy, who seemed to bring metaphorical glitter and rainbows—and even some real glitter and decorations—wherever she went, well… Maybe it was an unfair comparison. Poppy was one of a kind.

Abigail tapped on the keyboard, then clicked the

mouse to save her changes. She swiveled around in the chair to face Ryan. "A little revision, and that could work."

He looked down at the newly-rearranged elements of the slide on the screen. He had to admit, her edits made it flow better. Before he could study it closely, though, his phone rang.

"Oh, sorry, it's Zoe." He held up the phone, then swiped to answer it. "Yeah? Now?"

"Everything okay?"

Ryan laughed. He was surprised Abigail hadn't been able to hear Zoe through the small speaker. She'd practically yelled her message. "Yeah. I'll just be a few minutes."

"Okay."

She didn't say any more than the one word, but if Ryan didn't know better, he'd swear that Abigail was annoyed by having to share his attention with an eleven-year-old.

Poppy opened the oven to pull the pumpkin pie out. Earlier, when she'd put it together, she'd been so excited to share it with Ryan and the kids. This had been her Gran-Gran's pumpkin pie recipe. It had occupied a place of honor at Summerall holiday tables for generations.

But now that she'd also be sharing the pie with Abigail…Poppy thought about leaving it in a little longer. The crust would burn, and she wouldn't be able to serve it. She could make Gran-Gran's pie another day and share it with the kids. It would make a great after-school snack.

Poppy took a deep breath. That idea was dumb and childish. If Zoe had suggested such a thing, Poppy would have scolded the younger girl, and Poppy knew it.

She pulled the pie out of the oven and stared at it wistfully, thinking of what could have been if Abigail hadn't shown up tonight.

The familiar ring of her cell phone came from Poppy's back pocket. She looked at the screen. It was the Larsons' home phone number. The kids must be calling from upstairs. When she answered, Zoe breathlessly squeaked out the invitation Poppy had been waiting for since she and the kids had glued the last few sequins on the costumes before they went out to play in the yard.

"I'll be right there."

Poppy raced up the stairs. When she got to the master bedroom, Ryan was already sitting on the edge of his bed. He had his eyes closed and his hands over them for good measure. Poppy sat down and did the same.

"Okay, ready," Ryan shouted, loud enough to be heard down the hall.

Zoe called back to her dad. "All right. Keep 'em closed."

Poppy stomped her feet with anticipation. "The suspense is killing us!"

"Completely!" Ryan began to laugh at the same time Poppy did.

Right now, they were on the same team. They were both invested in these kids, in this moment. Poppy wished all the moments could come alive like this.

"Okay, you can open now." Zoe stood in the doorway, posing with her broom.

Her pointy hat sat jauntily to one side. The top of her black dress had been made with the velvet covered in purple stars. The skirt had been made of black tulle layered over purple tulle. Lace-up black boots tied with purple ribbon completed the look.

Poppy had loved every minute of pulling the whole costume together, but now, seeing Zoe in the full ensemble made her heart take flight. Poppy hadn't missed a Halloween since she was two—but never had she enjoyed being part of a costume reveal more.

"You look amazing!" Poppy's declaration seemed like an understatement.

Zoe continued to pose. She was fueled by sass.

"Beyond amazing." Ryan took Poppy's assessment one step further.

"I know. I mean…thank you." Zoe couldn't stop giggling. Her happiness filled the room. How long had this precious girl gone without showing off a Halloween costume?

Beyond the joy of seeing Zoe twirl and shine, a deep sense of gratitude settled on Poppy. She was thankful she'd been brought into Zoe Larson's life—and Ryan's and Zach's. She'd been brought here for a reason. She hadn't known why at the time.

Poppy knew why now.

She'd needed to find a way to commit to something, to prove to herself she could go the distance. But that wasn't why she'd been brought to this house, at this time.

These kids needed her. They needed someone to bring joy and costumes and cookies and holidays back into their lives.

Zoe changed gears to the next part of the presentation. She stood off to the side of the doorway, gesturing down the hall and made her voice boom like a ringmaster. "Now, introducing…the spider from your worst nightmares!"

Zach walked into the room, arms flying up and down. The movement made his other arachnid appendages bob and wave. He was dressed from head-to-toe in black, with a beanie cap on his head and gloves on his hands.

"I hate spiders! Who let that spider in here?" Poppy recoiled in mock fear.

Ryan placed his arm in front of her, defending her from the spider on the move. "No—no—no—no— nooooo!" He shooed Zach back. But instead, Zach took a leap and landed smack between Poppy's lap and Ryan's.

Poppy tickled Zach where he landed. She was so proud of him for his bravery in his choice of costume.

Only a few short weeks ago, he'd been waking up with spider nightmares.

"Hey, get in here!" Ryan waved Zoe in and pulled out his phone. "Group selfie!"

Zoe was game. "Okay!"

Poppy and Ryan squished close together and the kids leaned back. Ryan put one arm around Poppy's shoulder and she found herself instinctively leaning back into the solid support he offered. He stretched his other arm as far as it would reach. "Here we go. Okay…"

Everyone smiled. Poppy couldn't resist getting one more. They needed something crazy, a reflection of all the fun in this moment. Poppy wanted the kids to have a photo that they could look back on in the years to come—a snapshot that would make them smile.

"Silly!" At Poppy's instruction, everyone crossed their eyes and stuck out their tongues.

As Ryan tapped the button on the screen of his phone, Abigail appeared in the doorway.

"Wow, you kids look adorable."

Of course, she picked this moment, Poppy thought, deflating like a balloon. How many moments was Abigail going to ruin today?

The pumpkin soup seemed to be a hit—at least with four of the five people around the table. Poppy told everyone it was an old family recipe. Someone's family. Just not hers.

Everyone had a good laugh about the time-honored pumpkin soup. Except Abigail. She sat in her chair at the middle point of the round table, and barely nibbled at the soup through tightly pursed lips.

She'd ordered minestrone the other night at dinner, so Ryan didn't think she had an aversion to soup. Perhaps she had an aversion to pumpkin.

Or kids.

Or nannies.

In fact, Ryan wasn't surprised that the conversation quickly turned to nannying. He'd seen something simmering just below the surface since Abigail first sat at the table.

"So, how long have you been a nanny, Poppy?"

Poppy didn't take the bait. "Oh, a couple of weeks now."

"Really?"

"Poppy's nephews go to school with the kids." Ryan thought he'd try to help with a little clarification. Poppy was here temporarily by agreement, not because she wasn't qualified for the job.

Zoe took the opportunity to jump in. She and Poppy may have gotten off to a rocky start, but since that initial strife, Poppy had been elevated to hero status in Zoe's eyes. And she wasn't afraid to tell anyone. "Poppy's the best nanny ever. Nobody will ever replace her."

Hmm. Replacement. Ryan thought back to his conversation on the sidewalk with Abigail, where she'd assured him that they could work together to help the kids see that no one was trying to replace their mother.

It made Ryan pause. Poppy hadn't come in to replace Laurie. She hadn't even come in thinking she couldn't replace Laurie. It simply hadn't been on her radar. She'd just come in to lend a helping hand where she could and show the kids unconditional love.

Just like Laurie did when she was still alive.

Abigail had come up with an elaborate analogy and plan, and had she been given the green light, Ryan felt certain she'd have made a strategy and broken it out on PowerPoint slides. There wasn't anything *wrong* with that, exactly. But Poppy didn't need any of that. She didn't need a plan. She just led with her heart.

"Zoe—flattery will get you everywhere." Poppy's tone teased.

Abigail forged ahead. "So, what did you do before this?"

"Poppy can do anything." Ryan decided that Zoe would make a good litigator in court. She was issuing objections and clarifications like a pint-sized professional.

"Again, that would be an exaggeration." Poppy looked right at Ryan as she answered. She raised her eyebrows in mock protest and softened the whole look with a smile. Without even thinking about it, Ryan smiled back at Poppy.

Something inside told him Zoe's assertion might not have been hyperbole. In fact, it might just be right.

"Poppy made our Halloween costumes." Zoe paused, then went in for the kill. "By hand."

Abigail's eyes rounded like gumballs as she stuttered, searching for something to say. Ryan had never seen her at a loss for words before. Finally, she collected herself to say "That is very industrious. I do have to admit, that spider costume was quite scary."

"He's not afraid of spiders anymore. Poppy taught us how to face our fears."

At some point, Zoe's smugness had to wear out. How long could she keep this up? Ryan just kept eating soup. He didn't feel like he could correct Zoe—after all, he knew how much she loved Poppy. And she hadn't crossed the line into being actually rude toward Abigail...yet. In all honesty, he didn't know what he could say to rein her in. *Stop praising your nanny?* It sounded weird even in his head.

Ryan looked from Abigail to Poppy and then back again. This situation was rapidly becoming stickier than a popcorn ball.

Ryan decided he'd try to steer the conversation back to a more pleasant tone. "You know, I had a costume when I was a kid. It was so cool—I think I probably wore it four Halloweens in a row."

"What were you?" Zoe put down her spoon, waiting for the answer.

"A knight."

Zoe was intrigued. "In shining armor?"

"More like tinfoil."

Ryan's redirect worked. Abigail jumped back

in, seemingly more at ease with this dinnertime conversation. "My favorite costume was an astronaut."

"Really?" Zach finally spoke up and directed a question to Abigail. "What planets did you visit?"

Once again, Abigail sputtered before replying. "Well, I didn't actually leave Earth."

"But you're an astronaut." Zach leveled his assessment. He was not impressed.

"I think what Abigail is trying to say is that she went to so many planets that she couldn't keep track of all of them."

It amazed Ryan how Poppy always knew exactly what to say to the kids. No answer was too silly. No explanation took too long. Poppy just *got* them. And they loved her for it.

"Thank you, Poppy." Abigail nodded and made eye contact with each of the kids, as though to reinforce Poppy's reply as the truth.

Zoe decided to join in. "So, what was your favorite planet?"

"Pluto."

Ryan sat up straight in his chair. Zoe's class had just completed their space unit last month. He knew Zoe wasn't going to accept Abigail's reply.

Zoe folded her hands over her soup and rolled her eyes. "Pluto's not a planet anymore."

"Actually, that's inaccurate, Zoe."

Ryan knew this Abigail well. This was Boardroom Abigail. This was Negotiator Abigail who politely but firmly held her ground against any opposition. This was why he'd hired Abigail to be Parcel Technologies' consultant on the Food with Friends transaction.

This *wasn't* why he'd invited Abigail to dinner.

"Most experts say Pluto is still a dwarf planet. It's in the Kuiper Belt."

Zoe just sighed and picked up her water glass. Her silence said more than continuing the conversation could.

Ryan took in a deep breath. If this was Abigail's "merger plan" she'd spoken of for his family the other night, he might advise her to stick to Japanese tech companies.

"Are you going to be an astronaut this year?" Zach didn't pick up on any of the tension in the room.

Ryan envied his son right now. The woman he'd recently been on two dates with sat next to him. The woman he wished he could date sat across from him. And the young woman who had her mother's eyes was watching his every move.

This wasn't awkward at all...

Ryan looked directly down at his bowl of soup. At least the soup didn't judge.

Abigail replied to Zach. "Your father and I have a presentation, so we're going to be wearing business clothes."

"Yeah, it's a big day for us," Ryan agreed with Abigail. Circled on his calendar for months now, the big day was finally around the corner. Just one more hurdle and then he could make it to every trick-or-treat for the rest of his life.

Zoe turned the twinkle she'd been displaying up to a full spark. Ryan recognized that she wanted to make sure she had her dad's attention. "It's a big day for us, too. It's Halloween."

"That's right. And I will be home right after we're done." And not a moment too soon. He was looking forward to having the time to fully reconnect with his kids. His priorities had been backwards, but the minute the presentation concluded, they'd all be moving forward. Together.

Abigail choked slightly on a spoonful of soup. "Well, I hate to bring this up, but Higashimoto has asked us to be his dinner guests after the presentation."

Out of the corner of his eye, Ryan saw all emotion slide off Poppy's face. Her features went blank.

His heart sunk. He couldn't do this to his kids. "Oh…is that necessary?"

"It would be considered an insult if we didn't."

Abigail had put the final nail in the Halloween coffin. She'd made the point clear. He could either disappoint his kids or Higashimoto.

"Right. Okay." Ryan knew what he had to choose. He had to choose Higashimoto. Gathering candy with a witch and a spider—no matter how charming they were—wouldn't pay the bills and it wouldn't secure the future his kids deserved.

Poppy fell silent.

Zach fell silent.

Zoe spoke, as a line of tears formed in her eyes. "So…now you're not even going to be there at all."

She wadded up her napkin and threw it on the table.

Everything that one gesture implied punched deep into Ryan's soul. If Abigail hadn't been here, he could have told the kids in a different way, not just blurted it out at dinner. Poppy would have helped them all navigate it. It could have been okay.

But not now.

Zoe pushed her chair back and ran for the stairs. Zach followed closely in his sister's wake.

Ryan didn't blame either of them one bit. A tide of guilt washed up and pushed him from his own seat, calling after the kids. "Hey…both of you…"

Poppy turned in her chair and looked ready to run behind them.

"No, no. I've got it. I've got it." Ryan left both women behind at the table. Abigail would leave soon. Poppy was just under their roof temporarily. The damage from this would last far longer. Ryan knew he needed to fix it himself.

Poppy hadn't thought it could get any stranger after Abigail walked up on their dogpile after that tackle from Ryan.

She'd been wrong. Very wrong.

Abigail folded her hands and leaned on the kitchen counter. "It's funny. I talk with CEOs of companies. In Japanese. But talking with kids is a whole different story."

"Kids are like CEOs." Poppy finished washing the evening's dishes. She didn't have a lot of experience with CEOs—or kids, until recently—but she knew they shared several traits in common. "Except they're shorter. And smarter."

Abigail laughed, but there was no humor behind the expression. "You're really good with them."

"Oh, you should have seen our first day together. They barely spoke to me." Poppy lined the last of the glasses on the top rack of the dishwasher, losing herself just a bit in the memories. That first day seemed so long ago. "And I'm not even going to mention the hungry goat incident."

"Goat?"

"The thing about kids is—they're funny. And sneaky. Difficult. Goofy, clever, competitive." Poppy admired Zoe and Zach for being all of those things and so much more. "I mean, they're kids. So, they're lots of things. But they'll test you before they trust you."

Abigail nodded, but didn't speak. Poppy didn't know whether she'd said something right or something wrong.

Just then, Ryan reappeared on the stairs. "All right. Crisis averted."

"Oh, good. I'll get them ready for bed." Poppy looked forward to being back with people she knew liked her. It hadn't taken her long to get a read on Abigail's feelings. Poppy knew exactly where she stood there.

She stood on quicksand.

Behind her, she heard Abigail say "Well, I should get going. We can finish this up tomorrow."

"I'll walk you out."

Poppy had started out walking slowly up the stairs, but once she heard Abigail was leaving, she quickened her pace. That was all she needed to know.

The moon overhead shone brightly, scattering white light across the tops of the trees and giving a glow to all the decorations in the yard. Ryan walked with Abigail down the driveway to her car.

"So, I guess I'll see you tomorrow," she said.

Something about the tone of her voice sounded different, determined. Ryan wished he could put a finger on it. It wasn't the Abigail he'd known at work. It wasn't even the Abigail he'd gone out to dinner with.

"Bright and early," Ryan replied. *And not a moment too soon*, he thought. He needed a little time to sort out everything that had happened today.

"Good night." She stopped abruptly and turned.

With one sweeping motion, she reached up and brushed the hair behind Ryan's ear, then pulled up and touched her lips to his.

Ryan wouldn't have been more shocked if one of the ghosts had left the giant Halloween inflatable decoration behind him and then floated by. He hadn't asked for this embrace with Abigail, and he couldn't decide whether his reluctance was more because he was out of practice or because it was unwelcome.

Either way, Ryan knew he wasn't going to be kissing Abigail back.

Poppy had forgotten Zach's cup of apple juice in the kitchen. She ran back down to get it, but noticed the front door stood wide open. On her way back upstairs, she made a detour to close the door. They didn't need any real spiders coming in to test Zach's new-found resolve.

As she reached the door, some movement caught Poppy's eyes.

Instantly, she wished she'd let the spiders crawl where they may, because the sight in the driveway felt worse than one of Zach's bad dreams.

Abigail had her elbow curved around Ryan's shoulder. Her forearm brushed across his neck. And as far as Poppy could tell, Abigail's lips were giving Ryan a treat.

The only one tricked was Poppy.

She'd tricked herself earlier today into believing Ryan wanted to kiss her. She'd tricked herself into believing she wanted to kiss him.

Over the years, she'd had a lot of bad gifts tossed in her Halloween basket—toothbrushes, crayons, and that weird candy that sort of tasted like soap. But never had Poppy been given a broken heart.

Until now.

After Abigail drove away, Ryan went back inside and sat down at his laptop. For once, his heart wasn't in his work. And it definitely wasn't with Abigail.

Ryan knew where his heart was. His heart was upstairs reading bedtime stories. His heart was with Zoe and Zach.

His heart was with Poppy.

He tiptoed up the stairs and paused outside Zoe's bedroom door. The kids had made a tent out of bedsheets over the bed—probably one more project they could thank Poppy for. A flashlight glowed softly from inside the tent.

Poppy's voice was finishing one of Zach's favorite stories, *The Legend of Sleepy Hollow*. They'd been reading and rereading it for several days.

"'The very next day, poor Ichabod Crane did not appear at school. His horse was found wandering free. And so, the headless horseman was never seen again. The end'."

Ryan stayed silent in Zoe's doorway, listening to the conversation between the kids and Poppy.

Zach had heard the story a hundred times before, but he still didn't get it. "So, wait. He was really just a guy with a pumpkin on his head?"

Poppy made her voice sound low and spooky. "Or was he?" In a normal voice, she said, "All right guys, bedtime."

Ryan heard the sound of soft kisses gently laid on little foreheads.

"I love you, Poppy," Zoe said. Her words came out on a sigh.

In the dim shadow, Ryan could see Zach's form move over and snuggle up with his head on Poppy's chest. "I love you too."

"Oh…" The breath sounded like it had caught in Poppy's throat. "I love you guys."

He'd been right. His heart was right here in front of him. He loved his family.

All three members of it.

Ryan made extra sure that his footsteps fell silently as he walked back downstairs. He decided to wait on the porch for Poppy. He had something he needed to say to her. He wanted it to be private, just between them—not between them and two additional sets of ears who were staying awake to eavesdrop.

In a few minutes, Poppy came outside and closed the front door behind her. Ryan had been practicing what to say in his mind. As nerve-racking as the Food with Friends presentation was going to be, this one scared him even more.

But it also excited him even more—because this would change his life in ways that money never could.

"Hey, so…the headless horseman rides again?" *Just start casual, Ryan. Start casual.*

"And again. Zach wanted to hear it twice." Poppy zipped up her jacket. "Good night."

She looked off in the distance and stepped off the

porch. Ryan thought of the evenings lately when Poppy had lingered after the kids had gone to bed and they'd chatted over cleaning up dishes and other household tasks. Something had changed. Poppy's words held an edge.

"Hey? Can we talk?" Maybe she knew what was evolving between them as well, but was afraid he didn't feel the same way. That had to be it. She was nervous. Well, no problem there. He could set her at ease.

Just as soon as he figured out the right words.

And he had about forty-five seconds to do that—give or take.

She stopped halfway down the front walk and turned around. The orange glow of the Halloween lights strung across the porch sprinkled highlights in her auburn hair. "About what?"

"Us." He decided to keep it simple. But that didn't keep Ryan from feeling just as nervous as he did earlier today when he'd had to hold back from kissing Poppy in the pile of leaves.

"You want to talk about us?" Poppy's words were hesitant. For a woman who usually wore her emotions on both of her sleeves, she sure was playing this close to the vest.

"Yeah. Look, I—I know you were supposed to be temporarily ours." His feelings began to take over. Ryan hadn't experienced anything strong like this in a long time. A long, long time. "But, everything's just changed so quickly. What I'm trying to say is—"

Poppy jumped in to fill in the blank. "You want me to stay on as your nanny."

"Sure. Yes." But there was more to it, and he needed to let her know.

Poppy didn't let him. She started speaking before he could collect his thoughts. "The thing is, Ryan, the kids are going to get attached to me. And I'm getting attached to them. And that was never supposed to happen."

"Why not?" Megan had warned Ryan that her sister had a tough time committing to anything long-term. That had been fine when he'd only needed her to stay for a few weeks while he finished the presentation.

But now, why would she deny her attachment to the kids? Although Poppy's voice had been scarcely more than a whisper, he'd heard her upstairs loud and clear. She'd said she loved them.

What was going on here?

"Because you guys are a great family." Ryan could swear he saw Poppy bite her tongue before she continued. "And Abigail's here, and I'm kind of in the way."

Ryan couldn't believe it. Poppy thought he was falling for Abigail.

Was there an app for this? Ryan needed something to translate or make this easier. He felt completely lost. For the first time since Laurie died, he was putting himself out there. He'd definitely fallen for someone—but her name wasn't Abigail. "This is not how I pictured the conversation going."

"I don't think this is for me. I thought I could do this and not get involved." Poppy's eyes were devoid of their usual twinkle.

Ryan couldn't believe what he was hearing. "What?"

"I'll stay through Halloween, but that's it." She sounded so final.

Ryan felt his heart rate began to race. A tension knot formed right in the center of his forehead. "Halloween?"

"I mean, that was the plan." She reminded him of the agreement they'd made the first day they met.

Everything seemed as though it was collapsing around him. He had to make her understand. Maybe she just wasn't following what he was trying to express. He was a tech engineer by trade, not a motivational speaker. "Well, plans change, you know. People change. They get attached. My kids love you."

"And I love them. But I don't think this is going to work. I just don't—"

He could straighten things out, tell her that he wasn't going to pursue things with Abigail. But it wouldn't matter. She'd made up her mind. She wasn't staying. Not for herself. Not for him. Not even for the kids. And the kids needed someone who would be around.

More than that, *he* needed someone who *wanted* to be around.

Ryan was fighting a losing battle. And suddenly, he didn't want to fight—not with Poppy. He couldn't be her adversary.

"You know, I don't want to drag this out. If you want to leave, I think it's better you just do it now." Ryan began to breathe harder. He needed to rip off this bandage. Ryan knew his heart would bleed for a while, but as long as he could minimize the hurt for the kids, he could take whatever came.

Poppy looked as shocked as Ryan felt. He could see her swallow hard. "Fine. I'll swing by in the morning and I'll say goodbye to the kids."

This conversation had turned. It was no longer about him. It was about the kids. He couldn't protect himself, but he would do everything in his power to protect the kids' feelings. If the last words they heard from Poppy was the "I love you" she'd said tonight, that would be a good memory for them to end on.

"That's all right. I'll do it," he said.

"Well, only if you think that would be best for them."

"I do."

"Oh. Well, then…" Poppy shrugged. Ryan thought he saw tears in her eyes, but he couldn't see so well with his own eyes right now.

"Bye," she said, and hitched her purse on her shoulder as she turned for her car.

Poppy walked around the curve of the driveway past the decorations she had brought to life. She'd brought their whole house back to life. She'd brought Ryan's heart back to life. He wished he hadn't talked himself into opening his heart and embracing the changes he'd seen in his life and his family and deep in his soul. He wished he'd stayed in the lonely dad cave.

Because just like that, Ryan's dream of a family full of love and laughter died again.

Chapter Nine

Poppy sat at Megan's kitchen table. Sunlight streamed in through the windows, but Poppy felt cold. She'd stepped into a kind of perpetual shade. Everything that had been bright and purposeful in her life was gone.

"I can't believe you quit." Megan placed a cup of coffee next to Poppy.

"Ugh." Even caffeine couldn't fix this mistake. "I didn't mean to. It just happened. He asked me to stay on as *his nanny*."

Well, he hadn't said those exact words. Poppy had put them out into the air between them. But she only did it because she knew that's what Ryan was getting at, and she didn't want to draw the awful conversation out any further.

"So?" Megan seemed unconvinced that remaining as the nanny for the Larson family would be a bad thing. She sat down at the chair next to Poppy and took a sip of her own steaming mug of coffee with cream and two sugars.

"Well, I may not know what I want, but I know what I don't want." Poppy picked up her mug. She wished Megan had just left her coffee black. She felt like having something strong and harsh would better mirror the zigzag of emotions rolling inside her. "And that's to get hurt."

Megan leaned forward, almost getting into Poppy's personal space—but not quite. "Getting involved doesn't have to mean getting hurt. Come on, what happened to facing your fears?"

"That works for everyone but me."

"Poppy," her sister chided.

"I like him. Like, really like him." There. She said it.

And it hurt. Just like she knew it would.

Time to push away the tears she could feel coming. She forced her voice to not waver. "But I saw him kissing Abigail, so—I have to get over it."

"Maybe it was a friend thing?"

Poppy narrowed her eyes. Megan had to be joking. She'd clearly been living in happily-married-military-wife land for far too long. "Are you kidding? There's no Kisses with Friends. That's not an app."

"Yeah." Megan gave up the fight.

They both leaned back in the farm-style chairs and held their mugs.

With each stroke of the knife spreading peanut butter across the slice of bread in his hand, Ryan could feel the knot in his stomach tying up just a little more tightly.

Any minute now, the kids were going to come downstairs to head to school, and they would notice something was missing. Had it really only been twenty-four hours since they'd all walked to school together, holding hands and feeling connected like a true family?

Had Ryan only imagined it?

He knew the kids hadn't. He'd heard them each tell Poppy "I love you" last night at bedtime. But even though she'd repeated the words, Poppy must not have felt that love in the same way he or the kids did. Not for her to bolt and run like she did.

She loved them, but she didn't quite *love* them. There was a difference. And now Zoe and Zach were going to have to learn that lesson.

Ryan didn't want to be the teacher, but this was the tough part of parenting. He knew he must take the good with the bad. There had been so much good lately. He would focus on that.

Except all of those recent good memories existed because of Poppy.

Zoe stopped before she hit the bottom of the stairs. She looked around the kitchen and as far as she could see into the surrounding rooms. "Where's Poppy?"

Ryan tried to stay focused on the sandwiches. He didn't want his own emotions to betray him and make this harder for the kids. "I am going to be taking you to school today. And then afterwards, you're going to go home with the Marshall kids."

"And Poppy will pick us up from the Marshalls'?" Zoe's question was wrapped in skepticism.

"I am going to be picking you up, too." Ryan hoped he sounded convincing. He also hoped he could convince himself that everything was fine, that this was just the new normal.

Zoe wasn't buying what her dad was selling. "You're not working?"

"No, I'm going to work from home today. With Abigail."

"But what about Poppy?" Zoe wanted answers. It became clear she would not head out the door to school until she had an explanation.

Ryan understood why she kept questioning him. This abrupt change didn't make sense to him, either. But things were how they were.

Ryan decided to just level with the kids. Honesty was the best policy.

Zoe and Zach had stood tall in a lot of storms through their short lives. They would survive this too. "Look, guys. You know she wasn't going to stay here forever."

"But why not? She said she loved us." The words flew accusingly out of Zoe's mouth.

He didn't know if she blamed Poppy or him. But it didn't matter. Either way, he could see the fear and frustration rising up in Zoe, crushing her dreams and the joyful spirit she'd just recently reclaimed.

"She does. Of course she loves you two."

"She loves *you*."

At one time, he'd thought—or at least hoped—the same thing. But things had changed while Zoe had been sleeping. The whole world had changed. He'd gotten it all wrong. And now he had to tell his kids that Dad had made a mistake. A big mistake.

"I can tell," Zoe continued. "She talks about you all the time."

He wanted to tell Zoe that just saying it wouldn't make it so. But how could he explain it to her, when it didn't even make sense to himself?

"Okay. Look. I know this is confusing, and I'm sorry. But you've still got me, right? And I'm going to be here for you."

It was the best he could do right now. But he meant it. Even if they were just going to remain a family of three, he would always be there for Zach and Zoe. Poppy had taught him that, and it was a lesson he would never forget.

Poppy hadn't found her zen out in the so-called real world. In fact, all she'd found was disappointment and heartache. Megan had thought committing to something—going all-in—would be just what Poppy needed.

Megan was wrong. That kind of stuff worked for her minimalist, organized sister. Megan fit in perfectly as a military wife because taking orders and being part of a large, well-oiled machine suited her. She'd won awards in choir in high school and had made it to the state honor choir. She went to college on a scholarship. She'd met the perfect guy who had a passion for saving the world. They had the perfect kids and the perfect house and the perfect life.

Poppy wasn't perfect, and she knew it. She was rough around the edges. She liked new projects and the thrill of the unknown.

She had always been a free spirit. And just because that wasn't how Megan saw the world didn't make it a bad personality trait to have.

It made her Poppy. It made her able to relate to the Larson kids because she could be spontaneous and make messes and pies and jack-o'-lanterns and costumes.

Poppy swatted the thought of Zach and Zoe away like a pesky fly. The students at the yoga class stared at her, wondering if the lightning-quick hand motion was part of the closing of the day's practice.

Time to wrap things up before she confused everyone and they never came back. Poppy was starting to embrace her inner flibbertigibbet, but that didn't mean she didn't have bills to pay. She needed to build her clientele so she could turn this into a job with the rec center. "Thank you for joining me for what I like to call 'mellow frog'."

She gestured at her pose, then held her hands close to her heart and bowed, closing out the class. "*Namaste*."

"*Namaste*." The group repeated the salutation back to Poppy.

She hoped she'd been able to give them a little peace in their day—since she couldn't find much for herself.

"You came back." Her most regular student walked across the grass toward Poppy, carrying her tennis shoes in her hand.

"Mrs. Klemmer, yes, I needed a little bit of yoga."

The older woman had a thoughtful look on her face. "Well, that's good—I'm glad. But you were a million miles away."

"Why do you say that?" Poppy had worked so hard to flow through the routine at the right pace.

"I raised four girls. I know what boy trouble looks like." Mrs. Klemmer gave a knowing nod. Her bun bounced in agreement with the sentiment.

Poppy's heart sank. She couldn't hide. Megan had immediately interrogated her. Now Mrs. Klemmer saw straight through her. She was going to need to go into some witness protection program.

She needed to enroll in a Dejected Nanny Protection Program.

"Is it that obvious?"

The soft raise of an eyebrow spoke volumes. "So what did he do wrong?"

"No—nothing." Poppy leaned down to pick up one of her foam yoga blocks. "It's more complicated than that."

She couldn't explain it much further, because

honestly, she didn't quite understand it yet. Poppy hadn't fully processed the scene in the driveway. It was too fresh. She wasn't ready to relive Ryan's request or her response to it.

"Oh…sounds like unfinished business to me. And that's the worst kind."

"What do you mean?" Poppy could tell Mrs. Klemmer knew of what she spoke. Something inside told Poppy she needed to listen. And to take whatever advice came to heart.

"It follows you around wherever you go—unless you do something about it. Listen to your heart, dear. Don't take too long, whatever you decide."

Decide? Poppy had made her decision last night. And now, whether she regretted it or not, she had to live with that.

After sneaking off from the yoga class, Poppy sat on a bench at the edge of the park. Ducks waddled across the grass and waded into a lake. She drank in a deep breath of cool air and let it out slowly. Very slowly. In fact, she wondered if she could make time move at more of a crawl than it currently seemed to.

Why couldn't she have just been born a duck?

But she'd have probably messed that up too. She'd have tried to quack at the wrong time or been unable to march properly in a row. The truth hurt like rug burn on her soul.

Poppy had failed at a lot of things during her

so-called adult life. But she'd thought she was finally getting it right. She'd committed. She'd invested in these kids. She'd brought smiles back to their faces. And she'd fallen completely in love with them. Zoe's quick wit and Zach's shy side-hugs had made her get out of bed in the mornings before the alarm even went off.

And then, there was Ryan.

And then…there wasn't.

In spite of seeing Poppy every single day, in spite of pumpkin patches and cookies and family memories, Ryan had made his choice. He preferred the company of Ms. Quiet Italian Dinner. She probably whispered sweet talk in his ear in Japanese while they worked on presentation edits.

Yuck. The very thought made Poppy struggle to stifle her gag reflex.

Poppy rose off the bench and headed for her car. She began to drive without really knowing where she was headed. Her whole life had shifted back to some form of auto-pilot.

Suddenly, she looked up and saw a sign.

It had been placed over the road by the Washington Department of Transportation, but Poppy felt as though God himself had placed the sign just for her. She knew it in her soul.

Flipping her blinker on, Poppy exited the roadway and headed straight for the University of Washington campus.

A giant blue W welcomed her. Trees stretched down

the boulevard, reaching high to touch the branches of their counterparts directly on the opposite side. The leaves burned orange and gold and maroon. They looked like fire.

Inside Poppy's chest, a spark of that same fire flickered.

Her time with the Larsons had taught her one thing. She knew now she could commit. She could do whatever she set her mind to. And it was time to do more with her life than just bounce from one minimum-wage career path to another.

Ryan hadn't really been a knight in shining armor. That was just a costume. It wasn't reality. But that was okay, because she didn't need a knight to rescue her. She could do it herself.

Poppy parked her car in a visitor's space and walked into the registrar's office, ready to commit to her future. She would finish her degree and find her place in this world, wherever it was.

"Fine. You win." Poppy walked into Megan's kitchen and slapped her purse down on the granite countertop.

"Oooh, what did I win? I hope it was the Moolah Millions jackpot." Megan flicked a pinch of salt in a stock pot of water she was bringing to a boil.

"I discovered I can commit to something. I can follow through." Poppy pulled a folder from her purse and waved it. "So, I'm going back to school."

"You what?" Megan wiped her hands on her apron.

"Nannying was temporary. Ryan turned out to be a fantasy. This is reality. The University of Washington."

Megan plucked the folder from Poppy's fingers. "What's all this?"

"Information on degree plans." Poppy grabbed a pack of fruit chews from a nearby Halloween display. "I just need to figure out which one I want to do—I need to decide on a path."

"A path?" Megan looked down as she flipped through the pages.

"Obviously, all the math majors are out. But I figure I can find something I'm good at."

"Sure you can."

Megan was holding something back. Poppy could hear it.

"But what? Don't you think I can go back to school?"

Megan nodded. "Of course I do, Poppy. You're my little sister. I'm required by the sibling handbook to support you and to believe in you. And I do—I always have. But don't you think this is…a little sudden?"

"Nope." She unwrapped the candy slowly, then folded the wrapper into a perfect square. "I'm picking myself up, dusting myself off, and starting over. It's a new day and a new direction for me. You challenged me to commit. I did. It was Ryan who told me to go ahead and leave before Halloween."

"So, the next step is getting a degree?"

Poppy placed the candy in her mouth and chewed

thoughtfully. She wished she had something deep and philosophical to say in the moment. "Yup."

"You just don't know in what?"

"Well, I know what I'm *not* majoring in. I mean, besides math."

Megan pointed at the basket of fruit candies and stuck her hand out. Poppy obliged and placed two in her sister's palm.

"What?" The upward track of Megan's eyebrow was unmistakable.

"I won't be getting an 'MRS.' degree." That was for certain. She hadn't found her way to the UW campus today because she was looking for a fresh dating pool. All she needed was a fresh start.

Megan doubled over with laughter. "So, this is a bad time to ask you again about that guy I want to set you up with?"

"The worst, Meg." Poppy pushed the vision of a smiling Ryan at Rosewood Lane from her mind.

"But what if Ryan calls you back?" Megan popped the sticky orange square in her mouth.

Poppy wanted to say she'd send the call to voicemail. But she couldn't, because deep down inside, she knew that wasn't true.

She didn't need to spend any time chasing that rabbit trail, though. "It doesn't matter, Megan. He isn't calling. He isn't coming back. That phase of my life is over."

"Which is why we're so happy to become part of the Yamoharo Global family. May Food with Friends be just the beginning."

Abigail finished reading the formal remarks for the presentation aloud. She sounded in control. This was why Ryan had hired her to begin with. She knew just what to say and how to structure this deal to make it appealing to the investors in Japan.

"That's good," Ryan mused.

"We should add a line about how the app would strengthen the Yamoharo Global brand, right?" Abigail tapped the papers in her hand with the red pen she also held.

Ryan stopped typing, but didn't respond to the question.

"What's wrong?"

Ryan looked at the door to his home office, wishing he had X-ray vision so he could see through it and down the hall. "It's too quiet."

"Isn't that a good thing?"

In any other situation, Abigail's question would have made sense. But not in parenting. When it came to two kids on their own, after school, extended silence generally meant trouble.

"Not with my kids. I'll be right back." Ryan excused himself from the office and went to investigate.

"Sure," Abigail said, standing back and watching him go.

It wasn't full-blown destruction or scheming in the living room like Ryan had feared. Instead, depression had settled in like a spring fog, touching everything around the lower floor of the house. Ryan could feel the sadness.

Zoe settled back against the pillows and had propped her legs on the table. The board game Ryan had set up for the kids to play remained untouched—except for Zoe's feet on top of the stack of challenge cards.

Zach leaned on his own group of pillows and hugged his stuffed dragon tightly. He'd tucked into a ball and his head lolled to the left side. Neither kid bore any expression. Their faces were blank. Their eyes had glazed over, watching TV but seeing nothing.

Aside from the marked differences in age, gender, and coloring, they looked like identical twins. They looked like *miserable* twins.

"You guys okay?" Ryan asked the question, even though he already knew the answer.

Zach spoke up. "When's Poppy coming back?"

"Zach. Stop asking him. She's not coming back, okay? We'll just get another new nanny. Then another. Dad will always be too busy for us—so just get used to it." A lick of fire snapped in Zoe's eyes as she laid down the law for her brother.

Ryan sat down on the opposite side of the gray sectional from the kids. He addressed the kids directly. "Zo? That's not going to happen. Even though Poppy's not here anymore, things are not going back to the way they were. Okay?"

"Okay."

He could tell she only responded so he wouldn't speak any further. Zoe's one syllable offered resignation to the situation at hand, not agreement with what her dad was saying.

"I know you guys miss Poppy." Ryan took a deep breath. He wanted to reach out and hug his kids tightly. He wanted to show them they'd make it through this together. "You know what? I miss her too."

Ryan heard footsteps on the hardwood floor, heading in the direction of the study. He hadn't realized Abigail walked into the living room. But he knew she'd heard his heartfelt declaration.

When Halloween rolled around, Poppy threw herself into arranging candy. Filling bowls and strategizing how much to give each trick-or-treater somehow took her mind off of what she should have been doing.

She felt so stupid. She should have been putting the finishing touches on handmade costumes for a good witch and a spider—not separating out mini-sized chocolate bars from lollipops and taffy.

Poppy knew she'd messed up. Would it have been so hard to fight her feelings for Ryan? No. She could have done it. Those kids were worth the struggle. Those kids were worth everything to her.

But now, they were gone.

And Poppy had no one to blame but herself. Well, herself and her inability to commit for all seasons, to be there when things were uncomfortable. If she'd stayed with the Larsons, even though it hurt to see Ryan kissing Abigail, then she'd have been there tonight for the memories and the laughter that Halloween was sure to bring.

Even though she tried to tell herself she was excited about picking up the materials from UW, she knew it was just a Band-Aid for her emotions.

She should have stayed. She should have fought for what she wanted.

Poppy unwrapped a chocolate bar and bit off the end. Chocolate was all she had now.

"Ta-da!" Megan walked into the kitchen and twirled around. Poppy didn't quite understand her outfit. Shades of peach and salmon, with a padded X-shape worn tunic-style, the costume definitely was eye-catching.

Maybe it was a blinged-out Creamsicle. "What are you supposed to be?"

"Starfish!"

The tunic only had four arms. Nothing pointed upward around Megan's head. "Doesn't a starfish have more points?"

"I ran out of material." Megan gave an ironic spin.

"Well, you look very…aquatic." It was the best compliment Poppy could give, under the circumstances.

Megan picked up the boys' buckets off the counter. "Sure you don't want to come with us? Leave the bowl out with a 'please take one' note?"

Poppy couldn't go. She just couldn't. Seeing the neighborhood kids in their costumes…risking running into Zoe and Zach… No, her heart just couldn't take it. "I'm not going to risk having some teenager steal all the candy. I'm staying right here. I'm fine."

She would stay right here behind the door, toss some candy at kids, and then retreat from the outside world.

Megan didn't push any further, but gave a knowing half-smile to her sister before calling upstairs to the kids. "Okay, boys! Let's go!"

In seconds, the kitchen had been taken over by a great white shark and a purple octopus.

"Rawr!" Rob tested his best shark voice.

For a moment, Poppy remembered the fun of Halloween.

She laughed at her nephews and gave them a wacky wave. "Bye, guys. Have so much fun. You look awesome!"

"Thanks, Aunt Poppy! Bye." Steve ran for the door, his eight octopus legs jangling off the hem of his costume.

"Bye!"

Poppy reached in the bowl and stirred the treats around. Even the idea of chocolate didn't cheer her up. Her thoughts remained focused on everything she'd be missing tonight.

Poppy used to love Halloween. Now, it broke her heart.

She just needed to make it through this hurdle. Then nothing else would remind her of Ryan and the kids.

Except that she feared *everything* would continue to remind her of Ryan and the kids.

Jean, Ryan's office assistant, had volunteered to take the kids trick-or-treating after she saw her boss completely distracted. She knew she couldn't give the presentation, but she could at least take this off of Ryan's plate and ease his mind.

Ryan claimed he'd done pretty well at being a hands-on dad since Poppy left. But tonight, he had to enlist help for Halloween. Between tonight's presentation and a day full of final prep leading up to it, he couldn't be at the house and the office without the power of teleportation—but that would have been a completely different costume idea.

Jean wished she knew what had gone wrong with Poppy. From her view, she'd thought everything had been going well with the arrangement. Even Ryan had begun to slow his hectic pace at work. She'd been with him since Parcel Technologies opened its doors, and she hadn't seen him this relaxed since the year before Laurie died.

But a few days ago, all that came to a screeching halt and he went back to "panicked exec" mode.

And so, Jean found herself wrestling with eight black legs sewn onto a sweatshirt decorated with puff-paint spider web designs. "Okay, hold still. These arms are difficult."

"What is your costume?" Zach looked her up and

down, clearly unimpressed with whatever look she'd chosen.

"Uh…a harried executive assistant." Jean thought she might try her luck at a costume contest. No one would have a more accurate costume than that. She didn't just dress the part—she lived it. Especially the past few months, keeping Ryan organized leading up to tonight's main event.

Jean gave two final tugs on the costume, trying to get the stuffed legs to lay in place. "Okay, I think I've got it."

Zoe came around the balcony from her room. She summed up the scene in one quick observation. "I think it's backwards."

Zach lifted his own arm, making the costume arms underneath wiggle. The neckline on the sweatshirt gapped slightly in front. Jean walked around the back, giving the costume a side-eye. She pulled out the round neck-hole, looking for the tag in the back. Nope. Back to square one.

"Oh…uh…I knew that was too easy. Okay, let's go again."

At least Zoe had been able to put her costume on unaided. Plus, she looked sprightly and adorable.

Zach's costume, on the other hand, required an advanced degree in some technical subject. Jean sighed as she helped Zach tug off the sweatshirt. What *had* happened to their nanny? She'd made the costume. She should be here helping him get it on.

Jean wondered if she could ask Zoe to wave

her magic wand and get her brother's costume on straight—and to bring their nanny back so Ryan could start smiling around the office again.

The trendy industrial space gleamed with glass, light-colored bamboo accents, and stained concrete floors. Lights glowed, people mingled. Everything was about to happen. Ryan could feel the anticipation in the air. The scene looked something like a cocktail party before an upscale TED Talk for international investors.

He couldn't cage the butterflies in his stomach. So much rode on just a few minutes that would soon be here.

Abigail stood close by. She wore a plum-colored cocktail dress and had pulled her hair back into some kind of fancy knot hairstyle. She seemed elegant and classy.

Something inside of Ryan wondered what Poppy would wear to an event like this. He bet she could pull off the little black dress look very well. And as much as he loved the gentle brown waves with that little hint of gold that always framed her face, he thought she'd probably look amazing, all dressed to the nines with her hair pulled up.

He bet she would look like a princess. She did say she loved to dress up. Of course, she'd meant in Halloween costumes, but Ryan knew Poppy would be beautiful in anything she wore.

Even in a wedding dress. Especially in a white

dress with a thin, gauzy veil trailing behind her. His mouth went a little dry just thinking about it. And then a wave of regret flooded over Ryan's entire train of thought.

There was no use in thinking about what might have been. What was about to be was all around him—a deal with Yamoharo Global and a secure future for both him and the kids.

"So, this is it. When Food with Friends goes global, it's really going to open some doors for us." Abigail sounded nervous but excited. She kept looking around the room, making eye contact with people she knew and giving a small, dignified wave to each of them.

She'd been working the room like a pro since they'd arrived. Ryan, on the other hand, felt as though he was going through the motions. Smile. Extend a hand. Shake. Pretend like he knew how to speak Japanese. Exchange some small talk about his vision for Food with Friends. Then move on to the next person down the line and start the whole cycle over again.

"Yeah." Ryan looked down at his phone. Maybe Jean had sent photos of the kids. She'd said she would text him some candid shots from trick-or-treating. Seeing the kids would take his mind off the idea of Poppy in a veil and his whole heavy mood.

"And why aren't you thinking about any of that right now?" Abigail's tone chided him.

Ryan held up the smartphone. The screen was covered with a photo of a larger-than-life spider, grinning from ear to ear.

"Ryan, your kids will be fine. Okay? It's just one Halloween. They're going to benefit from your success. You know that, right?" She gestured to the crowded room as if to show him the world was at his feet.

International success was Abigail's dream. It was her goal, her "why."

Ryan's "why" wasn't any of that. Yes, he wanted to succeed, wanted to make enough money to provide security to his family, but he got up every day and created technologies to connect people, to make meaningful relationships easier to facilitate. And the two most meaningful relationships in his life weren't found here at this business event. His two most meaningful relationships were with a girl named Zoe and a boy named Zach.

"I do. I do—but they don't. It's just another night to them where their dad's working, instead of home with them. Again."

The look on Abigail's face hardened. She probably saw him as weak or unable to get his priorities in the right order.

"It wouldn't be so hard if I knew Poppy were with them," he said, looking at a photo of Zoe that had just popped up on his screen.

Abigail looked at her shoes and straightened her shoulders, then changed the subject. "I'm going to Japan, Ryan."

"You're what?"

"That job offer—Tokyo—I said yes."

"Okay." Unexpectedly, Ryan felt relief.

"I've seen you with Poppy. Your kids love her. And I'm pretty sure that you're falling in love with her too. I'd be fooling myself if I didn't acknowledge what was going on between the two of you, and graciously step aside. So…that's what I'm doing. I'm stepping aside." True to her word, Abigail took two steps back and walked off to the corner of the room, where a group of Japanese businessmen were talking.

Ryan didn't move.

If Abigail stepped aside, what did that mean for him?

Could he step forward? *Actually, no.* He didn't need to step forward. He needed to step backward. He needed to step back to that night in the driveway when Poppy walked away.

Chapter Ten

GIGGLES AND SQUEALS ECHOED OUT in the street. Poppy could hear the intertwined sounds of kids and joy from the other side of the closed front door. When the doorbell rang with the first group of candy-seekers, Poppy reminded herself to put on a smile.

She would find a way to enjoy her favorite holiday, no matter what.

"Trick or treat!" Two elementary-aged children asked for candy in unison as Poppy opened the door.

"Wow! Look at you!" Poppy admired their costumes and held out the candy bowl. "Here you go—don't be shy. No child left un-candied."

One of the girls was dressed as a skeleton. Her friend with braces smiled as she held out a pillowcase to be filled. Poppy decided not to give her a pack of gum. She didn't need any angry orthodontists showing up on her porch. "Hey, look at all those crazy bones. And you—your makeup matches your braces!"

The kids beamed with pride as Poppy admired their costumes. "Thank you," the girl said.

"Bye." Poppy waved as they walked down the porch steps.

She took in a deep, yoga-style cleansing breath. Okay, this wouldn't be so hard. *Just focus on the joy of others.*

Poppy could do that. There was so much joy in the world. She just needed to look for the good that was already around her.

Suddenly, a little witch came into view, walking up the sidewalk. Next to her was a little boy dressed in head-to-toe black. Poppy's heart leaped into her throat and got stuck.

They'd come! Her heart's dream had been answered. Poppy looked around—had Ryan brought them?

"Zoe? Zach? What are you doing here? I've been wanting to talk to you! Your costumes are amazing!" Poppy couldn't contain her excitement. The kids stopped at the door and gave Poppy a blank stare.

Poppy felt her face flush with embarrassment. These were other neighborhood kids. She had to explain. They probably thought she was crazy. "Oh. I'm so sorry. I thought you were my friends Zoe and Zach. They're about the same—are you in Mrs. Greene's second grade class?"

The boy shook his head no. Wordlessly, each kid held out a pumpkin-shaped plastic basket.

"Okay, you don't know them, but that's beside the point! We were all going to go trick-or-treating. Made costumes and everything. And their dad was going to be with us too. He really loved how they looked and he took selfies of all of us and we all made crazy faces together like a real family." Poppy continued babbling. "Anyway…you would totally love them. And their dad is the best guy I've ever met. He's kind and funny and…totally for me. Totally for me. He's for me."

The realization hit Poppy like she'd been slapped with one of Zach's spider legs. She didn't have to look for anyone else's joy around her. Joy like she'd never known before already lived inside her heart. She'd pushed it back into a corner, but it was still there.

Her biggest dream had been silenced by her own fear of being hurt, but it hadn't died.

Ryan was The One. And he was worth fighting for. Abigail would never love Zach and Zoe as much as Poppy did. And she would never love Ryan as much as Poppy did.

This time, Poppy knew she was a different person. She now knew how to commit, and that's what she would do—starting now. She was committed to fighting for what was in her heart. She would fight for Zoe. She would fight for Zach. She would fight for Ryan.

Ryan needed to know how she felt. She'd been so afraid of losing him—losing the whole family that she held so dear—that she'd simply turned and run away from the pain she'd anticipated. Poppy didn't face her fears.

The time to take her own advice had come.

"I—I… Here. Take this." Poppy shoved the whole bowl of candy at the witch. "I have to go. I have to go. Happy Halloween."

The room was filled with rows of chairs that seated about forty investors from both Japan and the local Seattle high-tech scene.

Abigail walked up to the microphone with poise. She'd done this before, and it showed. Ryan hoped when he stood in front of the group, he'd come across equally as confident.

"It is my pleasure to introduce you to Ryan Larson, a brilliant man who I know will be creating many more products for Yamoharo Global in the future. Ryan—"

Abigail extended a hand to Ryan, beckoning him to the stage area.

Ryan took his spot between two screens displaying the Yamoharo Global logo. He scanned the crowd and made deliberate eye contact with a handful of people seated in the front row. The pause gave him a moment to collect his thoughts.

"Thank you. First, I just want to say what an honor it is to be able to present this application to you all today." He reached in his pocket and pulled out a small stack of notecards. "Sorry."

Ryan flicked his eyes across the notes Abigail had written for him. There were details and bullet points. Through many rounds of edits, they'd both made sure that every question would be answered and every objection addressed during the course of the presentation. The goal was to leave everyone in the room with the feeling of *yes*. These were the executives and board members and financial wizards who would make this partnership a reality. Everyone needed to be on Ryan's side.

"I created Food with Friends because I wanted social media to be more…social. I wanted to connect people, face-to-face. So, imagine if you could sit down with a complete stranger and form a bond. Maybe you find some common ground and make a new friend. Maybe it's just a nice break in the day."

The executives in the audience exchanged looks with their neighbors. They weren't buying in. He was losing them already.

Ryan looked away from his cards. Maybe he could explain better with an example. "Okay, just imagine that out of the blue, you meet someone really interesting. Someone funny and smart who makes everything suddenly…better."

In the crowd, Higashimoto nodded, seemingly to himself.

Taking a deep breath in, Ryan forged onward. "Someone who sees the world differently and opens you up. Someone who reminds you of what really matters. That's the power of an application like Food with Friends. It can facilitate the chance meeting that could change your life."

Ryan stopped, then tucked his cards back in his pocket. Something else had taken root in his heart too.

He decided to speak candidly instead of segueing into the formal speech.

He could talk all evening about the power of connection and how it drove him to create the best product he could. But he didn't have all evening—not for the people seated before him. There was a much more important crowd that needed to hear from him. He needed to use this night wisely.

"You know, it's funny. I've spent all my time lately working on this presentation because I really believe—" Ryan gestured at Abigail, standing off to the side of the main audience group. "*We* believe—that Food with Friends will connect people. But as a result, I've missed out on time with the people I love most. Time I can't get back."

Ryan looked at the audience. He could see three people on the front row nodding along. As he scanned the crowd, pockets of other audience members had sat up straight. Others took notes.

He didn't have to give this presentation. Abigail knew the figures backwards and forwards. She'd nail the presentation. And if she didn't, if it didn't go well? He decided right then and there that he could live with it.

Nothing else would matter if he gained a fortune of money but lost his kids along the way.

"What I'm saying is that the only thing more important than making connections, is keeping them. I've enjoyed the chance to meet so many of you tonight and I know that once you hear what we've got planned for Food with Friends, you'll be as excited about the possibilities as I am. But for now, if you'll excuse me, I've got a spider and witch at home that want to go trick-or-treating with the only parent they've got. So, if you'll forgive me, I'll now turn it over to the insightful and generous Abigail Morwell to tell you all about this amazing application. *Arigato.*"

Ryan used the only Japanese word he knew. He hoped it would be enough.

As he stepped aside for Abigail—bringing their evening full circle—several members of the audience began to clap. And then suddenly, a wave of approval rode through the whole crowd. Ryan noticed Higashimoto reading the formal prospectus in his lap. He tapped his finger on a page of the small book and brought it to the attention of the board member sitting to his right. He smiled as they exchanged a few words.

They understood. Ryan could feel it. The energy in the room had shifted.

Now he needed to make one more shift in his personal life.

"I've got it from here," Abigail said, taking the microphone once again.

Suddenly, Ryan lost all twitches of nervousness. He was grateful for Abigail. She'd given him the last push that made him know once and for all that he needed to bring Poppy back into his life and the kids' lives. And not only had she graciously stepped aside from his dating life, she was now graciously stepping up to the microphone and stepping in for him, like a true friend.

"I know you do. Knock 'em dead."

Ryan headed straight for the door. As it closed behind him, he heard Abigail getting started.

"All right. Let me first thank Mr. Higashimoto and his associates for being here tonight…"

Ryan could barely believe it. He'd just walked out on what should have been the most important night of his life.

But it wasn't. The audience he needed to answer to was back at home. And the only investor he cared to impress tonight was the one woman he needed to invest in his heart and his family—forever.

Poppy paused and placed a large bowl of candy at the top of the porch steps. In front of it, she balanced a sign that read "Take as much as you want. Happy Halloween." She'd even added a festive flying ghost and a slightly awkward-looking jack-o'-lantern. Perhaps permanent marker wasn't her best artistic medium.

She could barely walk down the front steps, her mermaid skirt fit so tight. This would have been the perfect costume if she'd planned on remaining stationary tonight.

But she couldn't stay put. She had places to go.

There was one fish in the sea for this mermaid. And she was going to find him and reel him in, no matter what it took.

Ryan could hear a celebration starting as he unlocked the front door.

Jean let out a squeal of delight. "Ha ha! I think I've got it! I ain't afraid of no spider!"

"Trick or treat!" Ryan flung the door open. The sight of his kids with smiles on their faces made all the stress of the last few hours melt away.

"Dad!" Zach's eyes opened wide. He probably would've been less surprised if a tarantula had walked in.

Zoe jumped up and down. "You made it!"

"There's no way I was going to miss out on going trick-or-treating with you guys." Ryan folded Zach and Zoe into a bear hug, knowing he'd made the right decision. "Thanks, Jean—I'll take it from here."

"How'd it go with Global?" Jean seemed a little confused by Ryan's early arrival.

"Great. Abigail's wowing them as we speak." Ryan felt confident that Abigail had already closed the deal successfully. She wasn't the right woman for his personal future, but there was no one he trusted more with his business endeavors.

"Well, then, Happy Halloween. Have fun, kids." Jean picked up her purse and made a quick exit. She had grandchildren of her own, and Ryan knew she probably wanted to spend time with them tonight.

"Thanks again."

The kids waved and called after Jean. "Bye!"

"Okay, guys, listen up. I think I've got the perfect place to start trick-or-treating."

Zoe and Zach both smiled knowingly. They'd figured out Ryan's plan without needing to have it spelled out.

"Yes!" Zach pumped a fist.

Zoe stepped back on one foot. She eyed his suit and tie critically. "You are going to need a costume." With a push of her hand, she turned him toward the stairs and gave him a shove.

His costume wouldn't be as put together as anything Poppy created, but he knew the perfect theme. "I'll be right back."

The sounds of excitement on the first floor could be heard upstairs. Zach squealed first. "Eeeee!"

"This is the best ever!" Zoe agreed with her brother.

Ryan closed the door to his bedroom and slipped off his tie, throwing it and the suit jacket across the bed. Only a few days ago, they'd all sat together there, taking silly selfies.

He hoped many more family portraits would be in their future.

Was it possible that Ryan only lived six blocks away? It felt like six miles. Poppy's gold lame skirt had to be held up so she didn't trip on it. Criss-crossed strands of pearls jangled everywhere across the teal-sequined shirt that covered her chest.

Poppy dodged kids to her right. She dodged kids

to her left. "Sorry, guys. This tail wasn't made for swimming upstream." She searched every costumed child's face, making sure she didn't pass Zach and Zoe along the way.

"Excuse me. Sorry. Excuse me. Human fish, coming through."

The first day she met the kids, she'd tried to convince them she was a mermaid. Now, it was time to convince their father that she was his mermaid for life.

Ryan stopped at the top of the stairs and posed. "Well, how do I look?"

"You look great." Zoe gave him the once over.

Ryan had rigged two towels together like a medieval tunic, then secured another towel over his shoulder like a cape by way of a studded belt. He'd pulled Zach's plastic sword out of the playroom and taped a piece of metal wall art that Laurie had bought at a flea market to his chest.

Somehow, he knew Laurie approved of all this. He knew that she wanted him to live his life with joy and that she'd be happy about someone like Poppy guiding the kids and making them smile.

At no other time in the years since Laurie passed had Ryan felt this much peace and this much conviction about moving forward.

Zach broke Ryan's train of thought. "What are you?"

Ryan looked down at his costume. Okay, there

were a lot of towels. But come on, there was a sword. It should have been obvious.

"What do you mean? I'm a knight in shining—I'm your dad. Let's go."

In the greater scheme of things, it didn't matter whether or not his costume was easily identified. What mattered was getting to Poppy and righting the colossal wrong from the beginning of this week.

"We need our bags," Zoe remembered.

Ryan planned to stay out as long as it took to trick-or-treat their way to Poppy and to make her understand. Small baskets might not be enough. "Get your pillowcases—they're bigger. Go, go, go!"

As he shooed them up the stairs, the doorbell rang.

Ryan was surprised. He hadn't left the porch light on. A dim porch usually signaled to trick-or-treaters that the house wasn't manned.

Ryan opened the door anyway. He could find something in the kitchen to give one or two kids. Hadn't Poppy bought some kind of candy stash?

When he opened the door, Ryan thought it was a trick. Was he seeing a Halloween ghost?

No. It was not a ghost. The vision in front of him was definitely a mermaid. His mermaid.

Poppy stood on the doormat. She wore pearls and sequins and metallic everywhere. But none of it outshone the beauty that radiated from her heart. None of it flashed brighter than her smile.

"You're here." He couldn't say much, but those two

words summed up the only fact which truly mattered. She was back.

"*You're* here? What about your presentation?" The tone of her voice didn't give him many clues. She wasn't expecting him—that much, he could tell.

But was she glad to see him?

Or not?

"This is my presentation." Ryan gestured at the cuffs he'd made from foil and other playroom goodies of Zach's. "I've got tinfoil. I've got a sword. A towel."

Poppy laughed and took a step back, studying him from head to toe. "It suits you."

"I was just going to find you." It seemed important to let her know that they weren't just going in search of candy.

"You found me," she said.

He'd rehearsed for months to give a presentation to Yamoharo Global, and then he'd walked away because there was a set of remarks he needed to personally deliver before any more time scampered away.

Ryan would be winging this one, but he didn't care. Somehow, some way, he'd make her understand.

He just needed to start speaking. She needed to hear what was in his heart. If he kept it inside, she might misinterpret the signs again and leave once more.

"Poppy, we don't need a nanny. We just need you." This time, Ryan would make it clear. "I need you."

He left no room for misinterpretation.

"Really?" Poppy sounded like she didn't quite

believe him. He heard the hesitation and the uncertainty.

In the business world, people knew they'd been promoted when their job titles changed.

"How does 'Permanently Yours' sound?" Ryan could feel his breath catching in his throat as he tried to make sure the words came out.

Poppy shrugged. "Well, I mean, I'll need to make a new business card…"

"Yeah," Ryan agreed. It wouldn't be long until she'd need to change everything—her driver's license, her Social Security card, her passport… He'd see to that soon enough.

But first, he needed to make her "welcome home" official. Ryan reached out and pulled Poppy into his arms. This time, nothing was adjacent. Nothing would be interrupted.

He leaned close as Poppy tilted her head back. Lowering his lips to hers, Ryan felt just like a knight of old. He'd brought the princess back to the castle for the fairytale ending she deserved. Poppy stretched up on her tiptoes, kissing him back, and he pulled her tighter.

This was what happily-ever-after felt like.

Kisses with girlfriends.

No, scratch that. This was an amazing kiss with his future wife.

There wasn't an app for this—but who needed technology when you had the real thing in your arms? And this time, Ryan vowed to never let her go.

"She's back!" Zoe practically shrieked when she came into the hallway.

Zach's whisper was full of wonder. "She really is a mermaid."

"She's our mermaid," Zoe said.

Slowly, Ryan pulled back from the kiss, but kept eye contact with Poppy as he continued holding her in a close embrace. "Permanently."

Epilogue

One Year Later

"**B**RING THE PUMPKINS TO ME!" Poppy called from the couch early one Sunday afternoon after the whole Larson family had returned home from church. "The human pumpkin can't move!"

"You're gonna get pumpkin guts all over the living room, Poppy." Zach did as he'd been asked, but the look on his face showed a hearty dose of skepticism.

Poppy nodded. "Probably. But there's no way I'm getting up on those stools in the kitchen where you guys are. And I want to decorate too!"

She stuck her hand out toward Ryan, wiggling her fingers. She'd just had her fingernails painted last week and had chosen orange and black in honor of the season that had brought the most joy to her life. Without pumpkins and goblins, she never would have connected with Zoe and Zach and Ryan.

The first chapter of their story together was written

all around Halloween, and Poppy would never forget it.

Halloween had brought Poppy her family.

"As you wish, Mrs. Larson."

"Ooh." Poppy wiggled her shoulders—about the only part of her body that still could shake. Being forty-one weeks pregnant limited just about everything Poppy could do these days. "I still love the sound of that: Mrs. Larson."

Zoe hopped down from her stool at the kitchen counter. "Put on the video! We can pop some popcorn!"

Ryan sat on the couch near Poppy and turned to look at his daughter. "Don't you ever get tired of watching that video?"

"No," she said stubbornly. "I looked like a princess."

Zoe popped a DVD out of a case and slid it in the player. Romantic music began to play as the words "Ryan and Poppy's Wedding" flashed on the screen.

"Hey, what about me?" Poppy felt entirely certain that no one would describe her as a princess right now. Especially if they saw her ankles. Goodness knew she couldn't see her own ankles to judge for certain, but she didn't need to see them to know. She felt every ounce of retained water quite keenly.

Zoe flopped on the other side of the couch and wrapped her arms around Poppy. "You were a queen. A snowy ice queen."

"That's what happens when you get married right after Christmas. You get to marry a snowy ice queen."

Ryan placed his lips on Poppy's and gave her a quick kiss.

Far from thoughts of icicles, though, Ryan's kiss lit Poppy up inside. Every time he held her hand or kissed her, Poppy couldn't believe how fortunate she'd been this last year.

It had all started with an October kiss, but now she got to kiss this amazing man every month of the year.

He was hers. Forever.

Zoe snuggled close and Zach brought another pumpkin to the living room table. They were hers too. Forever.

And then…a little kick just below the ribs. Someone didn't want to be left out. Practically a honeymoon baby, this little munchkin had been ready to join Team Larson almost as soon as Poppy did.

They didn't know if Baby Larson would be a girl or a boy, but together, they would all be a family. Forever.

"*Ooof.* Hop off, Zoe. I need to move." Poppy tried to brace her hands behind her hips and lift off the couch cushions. The mere act of sitting felt as though it was cutting her in half. Maybe she'd be more comfortable on the floor.

Nope. She couldn't even shift positions.

She would be more comfortable not pregnant, and that was pretty much the only shift which would make any real change in her situation. She'd taken the fall semester off from her college classes to focus on her health and family. But all the prenatal yoga in the world was useless to a woman who'd passed her due date by a whole week and two days.

"Help." Poppy looked up at Ryan.

She could tell he was trying to stifle a laugh. So unfair. "I'm not laughing at you. I'm laughing with you. I promise."

Poppy attempted to press her lips together into a flat line before she spoke. "But I'm not laughing."

He threaded one of his arms around her shoulders and under Poppy's arm. Gently pulling upward, Ryan lifted Poppy from where she'd become stuck in between the cushions.

"A little more to the front." Ryan adjusted his own position so he stood in front of his wife, trying to scoot her over to a more balanced spot.

Finally, Poppy felt like she could use her arms and get enough leverage to push herself up to a standing position. She needed to get to a good place so she could prove Ryan and Zoe and Zach—and their skepticism about her abilities—wrong. She still wanted to carve pumpkins. Halloween wouldn't be the same without digging inside of a big orange gourd and then turning it into a work of art.

She shuffled herself to the edge of the cushions, locked her arms, and forced herself up a few inches.

As soon as Poppy stood, though, she suspected pumpkin time was over.

Pumpkin *carving* time was over. She was almost sure of it. But thankfully, so was her time as a human pumpkin.

"Hey, guys, I think we have a problem."

Ryan looked right in Poppy's eyes. "What is it?"

"I…think these cramps I've been having all day are actually contractions."

Ryan pulled his silver smartphone out of his back pocket.

"No, Ryan. No phone. Don't call anyone. And don't you dare take a picture of me right now." She sat down and sank back in the couch pillows.

"I've been working on a new app." He tapped and swiped a few times on the phone's screen.

"We couldn't, maybe—I don't know—talk about work some other time?" Poppy asked.

Ryan shook his head and turned the phone so it faced Poppy. "Nope."

Poppy read the words on the screen. A logo in colors of pink and blue and accented with a little rattle said "Make It Count."

"Make it count? What is that?" She sucked in her breath and gripped the couch cushion with her fingers. "*Ooof.*"

Ryan tapped the screen again. "It's a contraction timer. Did you just have one?"

"Most definitely." There would be no more denying what was stirring inside her body.

"Perfect."

"I don't know what your idea of perfect is, but…"

Ryan stopped Poppy before she said anymore. "I've logged that as your first entry. Now it will track how long your contractions last and how much time passes between each one. You can even rate them according to force."

He handed the phone to Poppy. The app's interface looked clear and easy to read.

"You made this just for me?" She sort of wanted to cry, but that might have just been because her entire abdomen felt as though it had just been clamped in a vise.

Ryan sat back on the couch and took her hand in between both of his. She loved how it felt, with her hand surrounded by her husband's touch. "I can't do what you're about to do. I can't even really help, except to just be here for you. But I wanted to make anything easier that I could. This way, you don't have to write the contractions down or remember times. The app does everything for you. All you do is tap once for a contraction and tap twice when it's over. It'll ask you to rate the intensity when it's done, if you want to do that. That way, you can see if they're getting stronger. I also set it up so that it will put the data in a spreadsheet and we can send it to your midwife so she can see your progress, too."

"That's amazing." Poppy felt a renewed sense of gratitude for this man. "Can you put it on my phone?"

Ryan stood and went into the kitchen, where he picked up Poppy's phone off the charging station on the counter. He brought it back to the couch, then held the phone back to her. "Just log in and I'll take care of it."

Poppy pressed her thumb to the button at the

bottom of the phone to unlock it, then took in a deep breath.

"Another one?" Ryan asked.

Poppy nodded, keeping her head down.

"Just breathe," Ryan said as he patted her on the shoulder. He tapped his phone screen once.

When the contraction ended, he tapped his phone screen twice in quick succession, then placed that phone within Poppy's reach.

"Give me just a minute and I'll have everything moved over to your phone so you can control the app yourself."

Zoe and Zach screeched back into the kitchen and held a stack of towels in Poppy's direction. Poppy took one off the top and dropped it on the floor between her feet.

Zoe looked at her brother, then at Poppy. "Wait. Is it time?"

Poppy smiled. It was hard not to draw energy from the enthusiasm on Zoe's face. "Getting closer."

"Kids, go back to your rooms and put clothes and PJs in your backpacks. I'm going to drop you off at Megan's on the way to get Poppy checked into the hospital. You will probably be spending the night, so take everything you need for tonight and for school in the morning."

For once, the kids didn't try to get in the last word. They went straight back upstairs.

"And don't forget your toothbrushes," Poppy

shouted after them. She realized she sounded like a total parent.

Well, she *was* a total parent. She'd been Zoe and Zach's stepmother for about a year, and there was no doubt in Poppy's mind that she loved them just as much as she'd love this newest member of the family who was now on the way. In a year's time, she'd gone from a woman who couldn't hold down a job at a pizza café to a wife and mother of three.

Well, mother of two-and-a-half, at least for now.

But not much longer. Poppy continued to tap the app on her phone as the waves came over her. She shuffled back to the master bedroom to change into clean clothes, then moved back to the couch and tried to prop herself up with pillows. As the clock ticked by, it became more and more difficult to find a position that didn't cause even more pain.

When the data collected by Make It Count showed her contractions coming steadily closer together, Poppy tugged at the sleeve of Ryan's dark gray sweater. "I think it's time. Will you grab my bag for me?"

Ryan didn't say anything. But the kiss he planted on her forehead spoke volumes.

He loaded the kids and the bags into their SUV, then came back to the living room for Poppy. Ryan slid an arm under her knees and one behind her shoulders.

"What are you doing?"

"Well, we don't have a wheelchair. I thought I'd carry you."

"Ryan." Poppy didn't know if she was more scared

for herself or Ryan's future chiropractic bill if he carried this plan through. "Remember that time when you tried to pick up the pumpkin at Rosewood Lane to get it in the wheelbarrow?"

Ryan pulled his arms back. "Um, yes."

"Just help me up. I can walk. I don't need a wheelchair or a wheelbarrow."

The next few hours blew by in a whirlwind. Poppy had elected to use the natural birthing suite at the hospital.

"When I signed up for this, I had visions of yoga balls and candles," she said, then blew a stream of air firmly out her nose.

Ryan held her hand. "We can get you some candles."

"I think we're sort of past that now." Poppy closed her eyes. "But some chocolate might be nice later."

"Chocolate. Wine. Roses. Whatever you want," Ryan said, giving her palm a gentle squeeze. "And maybe a new app."

"What?" Poppy almost choked on the one syllable, setting off the monitor behind the bed. Only Ryan could think about technology at a time like this.

"Wouldn't it be great to have an app that was like a virtual baby book? You could just carry it with you and log all the photos and milestones." He pulled his hand away and began to gesture. "And then—get this, we could get an interface so that you could print it out and bind it, all with a touch of a button. This could be huge. It would be every busy mom's dream."

"I think you're onto something, Mr. Larson," the midwife said with a chuckle as she shifted her position to the other side of the bed. "But we need to table the discussion for later. Poppy, I think it's time. Let's get you ready to meet your baby."

About an hour after dinner time, the door to the room flew open and a herd of little feet came running in. Zoe, Zach, Rob, Steve, and Megan all walked straight toward the bed in the center of the room.

"Is the baby here?" Zoe squealed and took pride of place right next to Poppy's shoulder. Zach squished in next to Ryan and everyone else circled at the foot of the adjustable bed.

Poppy pushed the button on the rail to tilt the back of the bed up a little higher. She turned her arm slightly and pulled the blanket corner away from the little face.

"She is."

"She?" Zoe's eyes went as round as the pumpkins they'd left behind at the house.

"You've got a little sister," Ryan said to his oldest daughter.

Zach stood on his tiptoes. "What's her name?"

"Autumn. Autumn Marie Larson."

"Autumn?" Megan said. "That's pretty. She'll be the only one in her class—and that's a good thing. I was always Megan S. so that the teachers could tell me apart from all the other Megans."

Zoe nodded her head. "I know Marie is Gramma Larson's name. But why Autumn?"

Poppy wiped her finger across her new daughter's soft, rounded cheek. It felt like an angel's wing. Poppy's heart was full. In fact, it overflowed.

"Because Autumn is my favorite season. It brought me everything I could ever hope for. You all became my family during the season of pumpkin patches and trick-or-treat and apples and changing leaves. Autumn has my heart."

Ryan stroked the baby's reddish-brown hair, which even seemed to embody the colors of the season. Poppy looked between her husband, their baby, and the two older kids who had stolen her heart. She was committed for the rest of her life, and nothing had ever felt more perfect.

"And now, Autumn is part of my heart. Just like all of you. You're permanently mine."

The End

Pumpkin Soup with Parmesan Croutons

A Hallmark Original Recipe

In *October Kiss*, Poppy is the nanny for Ryan's kids, Zoe and Zach. She can't help but be attracted to Ryan—and she sometimes suspects the feeling is mutual. So when he brings his sophisticated colleague Abigail home to dinner, Poppy isn't exactly thrilled. Nonetheless, Poppy graciously serves a savory pumpkin soup that Ryan and the kids adore. She jokes that it's an old family recipe—someone's family, just not hers. You'll want to claim this version as your own: topped with buttery-crisp croutons, shredded cheese, toasted pumpkin seeds, and a drizzle of crème fraiche, it's perfect for a fall gathering.

Yield: 6 servings
Prep Time: 20 minutes
Cook Time: 30 minutes

INGREDIENTS

Pumpkin Soup
- ¼ cup butter
- 1 small yellow onion, chopped (about 1 cup)
- 1 garlic clove, minced
- ¼ cup dry white wine (optional)
- 3 cups chicken broth
- 1 (15-ounce) can pumpkin puree
- 1 tablespoon brown sugar
- ½ teaspoon kosher salt
- ¼ teaspoon each: black pepper, grated nutmeg, and dried thyme
- 1 pinch ground cayenne pepper (optional)
- 2 tablespoons heavy whipping cream

Parmesan Croutons
- 3 cups cubed French bread (½-inch cubes)
- 2 tablespoons melted butter
- 1 tablespoon grated Parmesan cheese
- 1 tablespoon minced parsley
- ⅛ teaspoon each: kosher salt and black pepper
- ½ cup crème fraiche*

- 6 slices bacon, cut into ½ inch pieces, cooked until crisp
- ¼ cup shaved Parmesan cheese
- 3 tablespoons toasted pumpkin seeds

DIRECTIONS

1. Preheat oven to 400°F.

2. **To prepare pumpkin soup:** melt butter in a large heavy saucepan over medium heat until butter is foamy and turns a light golden brown (about 2 minutes). Add onions and garlic; saute over medium heat for 5 minutes, stirring frequently.

3. Add white wine and simmer for 2 minutes, or until liquid has reduced. Add chicken broth, pumpkin puree, brown sugar, salt, black pepper, nutmeg, thyme and cayenne pepper; stir to blend. Simmer for 10 minutes or until fully heated. Remove from heat.

4. Working in several smaller batches, puree in a food processor fitted with a steel blade or blender until smooth. Return mixture to saucepan. Add heavy cream and simmer over low heat until fully heated. Taste and adjust seasoning, if needed. Keep warm.

5. **To prepare Parmesan croutons:** combine bread cubes and melted butter in a large bowl and toss to coat. Add Parmesan, parsley, salt and black pepper; toss to blend. Transfer to baking sheet lined with parchment. Bake for 10 to 15

minutes, or until light golden brown, stirring halfway through baking. Set aside.

6. **To serve:** ladle soup into bowls. Top each with a drizzle of crème fraiche, Parmesan croutons, crisp bacon pieces, shaved Parmesan cheese and toasted pumpkin seeds.

*If you'd like to make your own crème fraiche, simply put 1 cup whipping cream into a glass bowl and add 2 T. buttermilk. Cover and let stand at room temperature for 8-24 hours. Refrigerate any unused portion for up to two weeks.

Thanks so much for reading *October Kiss*.
We hope you enjoyed it!

You might like these other books
from Hallmark Publishing:

Journey Back to Christmas
Christmas in Homestead
Love You Like Christmas
A Heavenly Christmas
A Dash of Love
Love Locks
The Perfect Catch
Like Cats and Dogs
Dater's Handbook
Christmas in Evergreen

For information about our new releases and
exclusive offers, sign up for our free newsletter at
hallmarkchannel.com/hallmark-publishing-newsletter

You can also connect with us here:

Facebook.com/HallmarkPublishing

Twitter.com/HallmarkPublish